I0517514

The Painter

The lure of social media—
instant love!

**Elizabeth Stitchway, PI, Series
Book 3**

MARY JANE FORBES

Todd Book Publications

In memory of

Richard Colton
my brother-in-law...

...who painstakingly read through my first drafts
with patience and laughter.

He was one of the good guys.

The Painter

The lure of social media—*instant love!*

Prologue

—

HER PALE FINGERS SHOOK as she parted the sheer curtains a crack and gazed down at the idyllic scene—paradise! Spring buds on the trees were turning apple green. A duck bobbed on the water of the man-made canal flowing in back of the house. He stuck his bill into the water, then his whole body lurched for a fish—a morning delicacy.

The sheer fell back into place. The woman looked around the elegant bedroom—pale-lavender walls, ice-blue quilt made of satin, lace, and ribbons. A white-lattice partition created a cozy, private alcove for her antique French desk. Her eyes lingered over the floor-to-ceiling bookcase stuffed with books of all sizes and bindings. Books were piled two deep alongside the shelving as well as under the bedside table—books where she became the heroine only to return to her depressing life. The disorderly books stood out in an otherwise orderly room. This room was nothing like the rest of the house—sterile white.

I'm that fish under water waiting to be eaten, she thought.

It was all her husband's fault. Everything was his fault. She was a prisoner in this Florida paradise. Her eyes misting, she felt the gray curtain of despair descend over her.

No. No. Not today. Seizing the telephone on the bedside table she quickly tapped the familiar numbers before she lost the will to reach out for help.

"Hello," a woman's voice answered on the other end.

"Mom, it's me … Vivien."

"Oh, my, Viv. It's been so long. Months. How are you, dear?"

"I'm fine," she whispered. "How are you?"

"It's raining sheets. So what else is new in San Francisco," she chuckled.

Silence filled the connection.

"Vivien, you don't sound fine. Tell me."

"Nothing really. Kelly turned sixteen last month, Valentine's day."

"I know. I wanted to wish her a happy birthday, at least over the phone. Did she get my present? The silk scarf? I thought it was so pretty. Very grown up."

"Yes, it came … she loves it. I can't really talk now, Mom. Just needed to hear your voice."

"Vivien, this isn't the number you usually call me from. Are you—"

"Oh, my God. I messed up." Vivien slammed the receiver down in the cradle, jerked her hand back, her fingers burning. She stared at the instrument. Her breathing stopped. Flinging herself on the bed, she curled into a ball, her jet black hair sprawling over the satin pillow sham muffling her sobs … catching her tears.

———

HEAVY FOOTSTEPS ECHOED off the cement-block walls as the guard approached the prisoner's cell. Keys clanked against the bars. The guard lifted the heavy metal bolt.

"Steele, you have a phone call. Something about your release. The Warden said you could take it, seeing how you ain't been using your phone privileges lately."

Steele laid the thick sketchpad down on his bunk at the same time kicking a carton of drawings to the side. He put his hands out. Cuffs were locked around his wrists. The prisoner named Steele— black hair and beard, taut muscles hidden under his prison garb, grim-faced followed the guard back down the center of the row of cells.

Inmates started banging tin cups against the bars, shouting at Steele to grab the keys, but he kept his eyes straight ahead—picture of a model prisoner. He was due to get out of this hell hole in three months. Over the past eleven years, he had learned to keep his temper and emotions tamped down, to keep his mouth shut, no fighting, do what he was told. On the outside, his demeanor appeared tamed. Inside his blood boiled with hate.

If he had a phone call, then he had a phone call. About time. Pit Bull was supposed to have called last week with the arrangements for the day of his release.

Steele picked up the receiver dangling beneath the wall phone.

"Yea?"

"Took your sweet time getting to the phone, Razor."

"I had to walk through the tulips. Where've you been? I've been waiting."

"Is this phone secure?"

"No. You're being piped into Disneyland. Why do you always ask me that? Are you using a disposable phone?" Razor asked, leaning against the wall and sliding down to sit on the cement floor.

"Of course."

"Talk ... then throw it in the ocean."

"I know what to do. I called about that Babcock guy."

"And. What about him?"

"Remember you said you saw a news article ... on that computer you play with ... the story about a company buying a new design from an unknown scientist? A computer scientist. You thought maybe we should put another tap on the mother-in-law's telephone.

"So."

"So, the daughter called her not more than an hour ago only this time she called from another phone. I think it was her home phone."

Razor stood up. "Now, there's a piece of good news. Have you traced it yet?"

"Hey, what do you think? Of course, I traced it."

"To where?"

"Daytona Beach."

"Florida?"

"It's the only one I know of. This gives you something to search for—you know, the internet. I'll have more when you get out. Then we can put our plan into action. Her husband's not going to know what hit him."

Chapter 1

—

Three Months Later

POLLY SURVEYED THE FLOWERBEDS circling her backyard enjoying her second cup of coffee in the rays of the morning sun. Resting in her lawn chair, she jotted down another item on her list of garden chores. The list had grown to two pages so she had to prioritize or some of the plants would surely die from neglect.

She leaned back, mulling over the day ahead. Friday. Not just any Friday but the once-a-month quilting-group Friday.

"Why did I ever start this quilting thing, Regina?" Regina, a Shih-Tzu mix Polly rescued from the shelter, looked up at her mistress with adoring, big black eyes, and a little whine in response to the question posed to her. Polly gave a pat on her little head. They both looked up sharply at the sound of a squirrel scrambling along the branches of the oak tree, an acorn treat clamped in its mouth.

"You know very well why," she said to Regina. "It was the website that popped up when I searched for *quilts*. 'Quilts of Valor—sew a keepsake for a wounded warrior.' God knows they deserve our gratitude. It's not that I don't enjoy the girls once they get here, but—"

Regina raised her paw asking for another pat.

Polly obliged her pet and turned the page on her notepad to start another list of what had to be done before the quilters arrived. Blowing a warm, moist breath of air on her glasses, she wiped them with the bottom of her peach T-shirt and slipped them back through her short silver waves.

The squirrel had moved on but a pair of ducks floated into view enjoying the cool water gently flowing in the canal. Polly and her late husband loved to watch various wildlife dip in and out of the water, especially now in the middle of June when the air reached into the eighties in the afternoon. He'd been gone three years and Polly was feeling a bit lonely without her husband—dinner out, plays, the concerts. There was a man at church, three pews up—he always sat alone, but she didn't approach him. He was probably content with his life she surmised.

Last night Polly had watched a program about meeting people on the internet—dating sites they called them. She jotted down two of the website addresses. *Maybe I'll ask the girls today what they think?*

Polly took her coffee mug and notepad, with several pages of to-do entries, into the kitchen and set about preparing the dining room for her quilter friends. Regina jumped to her feet, prancing along with her mistress in hopes of a doggie treat.

Polly's house, in a friendly Daytona Beach development, Pelican Bay, was perfect for the quilters. The dining-room table, expandable, now open to its full eight-foot length, allowed each quilter a side to move back and forth freely stitching the top fabric to the bottom through the padding in the middle. A galley kitchen was concealed behind a wall separating it from the living and dining rooms. All painted in sugar-cream and open to a view through sliding glass doors of the lawn, gardens, and canal beyond.

Two of the quilters were neighbors—Mildred a fifty-two-year-old spinster and Kelly, sixteen, with a big heart, who warmed immediately to the idea of adding her stitches to the quilt.

Susan, a socialite who called a mansion on the beach overlooking the Atlantic Ocean home, was the fourth member of the group. Her pretty cap of rich-brown hair framed her face which always appeared as if she had just sucked a lemon wedge. She heard of the quilters through her stockbroker's receptionist one day while waiting for her appointment. She thought she might try her hand at the cause. It certainly couldn't hurt to join for a few sewing sessions and would add a certain cachet to her standing in her circle of friends—something to talk about over lunch at the country club after a round of golf.

———

THE SOUND OF SCISSORS snipping thread accompanied a deep sigh. The three other quilters looked up from their sewing.

"What's the matter, Polly?" Mildred asked. "You don't seem yourself today."

"Just restless, I guess. The London Symphony is performing in a couple of weeks. I wish I could go."

"My mom loves the symphony," Kelly piped up. "I bet she'd go with you. She's seemed a little down lately. It would be nice for both of you." Flipping her silky-black ponytail, she smiled over at Polly.

"With a man." Polly pierced the cotton fabric with her needle and yanked the thread through.

"For heaven's sake, you're seventy-two," Susan quipped. "Do as Kelly suggested. Invite her mom to accompany you."

"I want to find a male escort ... for more than the symphony."

"You mean an affair?" Susan asked holding her needle midair, eyebrows rising. "Sex? You're nuts. Kelly, hand me that spool of thread. No, not the blue, the red. Really, Polly. Next thing you're going to tell us is that you've signed up on one of those internet dating sites like eHarmony. As if dating is harmonious."

"Well, I have thought about it. But I suppose you're right. I'm too old for that stuff."

Mildred had held her tongue. Listening. She'd had trouble with relationships and knew people called her a spinster. Her flowered house dress, under a yellow apron around her waist, covered her ample body. "It might be worth a look," she said keeping her head down. "After all, it doesn't hurt to look. See who's out there? No harm in—"

"Harm?" Susan snapped. "She could be raped, robbed ... I dare you, Polly Pringle. I dare you to do such a foolhardy thing."

The quack of a duck sprang from the cell phone lying on the quilt in front of Kelly. Grabbing her phone, holding it to her ear with her shoulder, she continued stitching.

"Carol, I can't talk now. What? Wow. Bye." Pushing her needle into the fabric, Kelly freed her hands and quickly poked her cell's keypad with both thumbs moving in a flurry. She smiled, closed her phone, laid it back on the quilt, and pulled her needle through the stitch. Feeling the stares of the others, she looked up. "What?"

"Honestly, Kelly," Susan said. I don't know how you can concentrate on quilting. You're always on that thingamajig—"

"Cell phone. And, I'm not always on it. Look, I've—" She was interrupted by a quack, quack. Grabbing for the cell, she pricked her finger on the end of her needle.

"Ouch!"

Polly jumped up sending Regina flying off her lap barely landing on her feet. Polly grabbed Kelly's finger. "Don't drop blood on the quilt," she yelped, dragging Kelly to the kitchen sink. She turned on the cold water pushing Kelly's finger under the faucet. "Hold it right there, sweetie, while I get a bandage."

"Thanks, Mrs. P. Susan, I didn't get any blood on the quilt did I?" Kelly shouted from the kitchen.

"No. A little drop on the table. That'll teach you to put that phone away." Susan picked up the cell which had stopped quacking and dropped it into Kelly's backpack hanging over the back of her chair. "So, Polly, are you going to take us up on our dare?" she called out.

Polly returned with a bandage, dried Kelly's finger, and took the band-aid out of its wrapper. "What do you mean, our dare?" she asked. "There, Kelly, that should stop the bleeding."

"We three—me, Mildred, and Kelly dare you to put a man-wanted ad on one of those personal sites," Susan said staring into Polly's eyes as she returned to the table. "You should try Senior Friend Finder—given your age," Susan said. "Of course, you don't look elderly."

"Susan, that's not very nice," Mildred said. "But, Polly, if you do, you should prepare."

"What do you mean prepare?" Polly asked, taking her seat across from Kelly. She picked up her needle and took a stitch as Regina hopped up and once again settled herself on Polly's lap.

"That's a good idea, Mildred," Susan said. "You definitely need a cell phone, better yet, one of those smartphones."

"What's so smart about it," Mildred asked, pulling her needle through the fabric.

"Takes pictures. Tells me what movies are playing," Kelly said. "I can talk or text. Get the newspaper whenever I want. Oh, and go to my school's website for class assignments. Lots of stuff."

"And Polly can call for help if she meets up with Jack the Ripper," Susan added laughing.

"That's what I mean by prepare," Mildred said. "In case she meets up with Mr. Ripper, she'd better take a self-defense class. The police department runs classes every month. In fact, we could all go with you. A woman can't be too careful these days. You too, Kelly. Pretty young girl like you should arm herself."

"So?" Susan asked.

The three quilters stopped needles mid-air, waiting for Polly's reply.

"Well, I guess it wouldn't hurt to look at a dating site, and a self-defense class would be fun if all four of us went, but you have to promise at least one of you will come with me."

"And," Kelly said, taking a stitch, "I'll help you pick out a cell phone."

"Oh, I have a cell. What? You think I'm not hip?"

Chapter 2

———

Sacramento, California

THE SUN WAS SHINING as Razor stepped outside onto the sidewalk of Folsom State Prison. The iron gate, an opening in the granite wall topped with curling barbed wire, banged shut. A young man, yellow curls fringing his ball cap, followed a step behind Razor. Both stood still a moment, breathing in the fresh, free air. The Warden had given Razor the few items he had in his pockets, including $50.63, when he entered the prison eleven years ago.

A shiny-white SUV pulled to the curb next to the grassy slope and stopped. The driver kept the motor running as he flicked a cigarette butt out the window. Razor walked quickly to the vehicle, calling over his shoulder for the young man to sit on the bench by the bus stop.

"Uh, okay, Razor," he said shuffling over to the bench. He kept looking around to see if Razor was leaving him behind.

Razor opened the door of the car, slid onto the front seat nodding to the driver. Buddy Brown otherwise known as Pit Bull, fifty-three, bald with a stomach that preceded him, sat behind the wheel. Neither said a word. Bull pulled an unaddressed, plain-white envelope from the breast pocket of his black cashmere jacket, handing it to Razor, the sun's rays through the windshield bouncing off of Bull's diamond ring and heavy gold necklace. Razor always thought the moniker, Pit Bull, fit him—short, big jowls and treacherous—an attack dog that could kill someone he didn't like in the blink of an eye. A scar running from his right ear to the bottom of his cheekbone verified he could fight and live to see another day.

Razor carefully slit the top flap, spread two fingers inside the envelope, opening it enough to peek in and verify the contents. He slowly released his breath as he counted the large bills—$1,650,000—his pay of $150,000 a year for the past eleven years.

"You look good, Razor, except for the hair," Bull said. "A little pasty, but a few months under the Florida sun will fix that. What's with the kid?"

"His name is Lenny. The dumb-ass thought he could hold up a 7/11 with a toy pistol. He had a couple of priors so they gave him a year in the can to convince him he shouldn't play cops and robbers."

"And, did they?"

"You kidding, Bull? Once a punk always a punk. Anyway, I thought he might come in handy. First of all, he can help with the drive to Florida. After that … well, I'll see."

"Did you make contact with the woman?" Bull asked.

"Sure. Once you came up with the name it was easy. I couldn't crack her email address but I did find her on FaceBook. They have this private message feature so she and I have been corresponding over the last three months—always inside FaceBook."

"You make any move to meet her?"

"No. I figured I'd wait until I was in Florida. But we've become quite chummy and I think she'll agree … once I ask."

"So you have a plan?"

"Oh, yea. I have a plan."

A dusty Greyhound bus rolled to a stop at the curb emitting a belch of fumes with a hiss as the driver applied the brakes. Four women wearing somber faces stepped off the bus and headed for the gate. Lenny looked over at Razor. Was he supposed to take the bus? Razor flagged him to come to the car. Lenny shuffled over, hesitated, then stopped short about two feet away. He did not move to open the back door.

"Drop me off at the Sacramento airport," Bull said. "It's about thirty minutes down the highway. There's a suitcase with clothes—a blazer, couple of black micro-fiber trousers. Figured you'd appreciate something soft after the prison garb you've been wearing. And, of course, those Italian leather shoes you like."

"What about the two cartons I sent. Are they in the back?"

"Yep, and you'll also find a cell phone, plus a couple of disposables, a laptop, and a Glock with a box of ammo. There's a map in the glove compartment if you need it. Your contact's telephone number and address are in the envelope along with the money."

"Billy?"

"Yep. Good old Billy," Bull said with a smirk.

Bull hit the button and the backdoor lock flipped up. Razor nodded his head indicating that Lenny should climb in. Razor didn't introduce Bull. He kept his eyes straight ahead on the grassy slope. He had no stomach to look at the granite structure with its pigeon-hole windows ever again. Bull lit a cigarette, took a drag, then eased away from the curb and was soon on Highway 50 to Sacramento International Airport.

The vehicle sped down the highway. There was no conversation—the three men lost in their own thoughts. Seeing an airport sign indicating they were within five miles, Bull lifted a finger from the steering wheel that that was where he would part company with Razor and Lenny.

Lenny broke the silence. Sitting on his hands, he rocked back and forth on his seat, looking out the window. "Nice day," he said.

Razor glanced around at the kid—his cellmate for the past year. He was twenty-three. A punk. When Lenny asked if he could tag along with him for awhile when they were released, being as they were scheduled to get out on the same day, Razor had agreed.

"Yea, Lenny, it's a nice day."

"Where are we gonna spend the night, Razor?" Lenny asked.

Razor fished around in the glove compartment and retrieved the map Bull had put there for him. He unfolded the map to show the western third of the United States and traced the highway with his finger traveling south in California, and then picking up I-10 toward San Bernardino and swinging east to Arizona, New Mexico and Texas.

"We should be able to get as far as Santa Ana."

———

LEAVING THE SACRAMENTO Airport, Razor waved goodbye to Bull and merged onto I-5 South.

"You still think you can get me a job, Razor? When we get where you're going? You never said where that was. Where you … where we're going? I only have thirty-four dollars and a few pieces of change."

"Daytona Beach, Lenny. Warm, sunny, Daytona Beach. That's where we're going. They say it's like paradise. I said I'd help you for a couple of weeks. Then you're on your own." Razor looked out his window at the lush California landscape. He felt good, rolling down the highway behind the wheel of a brand new SUV.

He thought back to the fateful day he and Bull were visiting a company Bull had invested heavily in through various front men. Bull had told him to wait in the conference room. Razor heard a gunshot and the next thing he knew, Bull barged through the conference room door throwing him a package. "Say you're the delivery man," he yelled. "I'll make it up to you." That's all he said and then he disappeared.

Razor learned that one of the principals of the firm was shot dead. For awhile the cops thought they had their man—Razor. But the evidence pointed elsewhere. Bull was no fool. He had insurance. He had planted a shipment of drugs in Razor's car and home—easily found when the cops discovered him holding a package of coke, causing them to search him further. The wrapping and purity of the powder pointed to a Mexican cartel pushing up the California coast. The officers tried to break Razor, make him finger the top man, maybe he knew who committed the murder, but he stuck to his story—he knew nothing. He had never been in the building before. He was just a messenger, delivering the package to the company. He never met the person who gave him the stuff. He was only told where to pick it up and where to deliver it. The Feds didn't buy his story. As far as they were concerned they had the leader of the drug ring, at the very least, the next in charge.

After Razor was incarcerated, he had a visitor who let him know Bull would be in touch and he would make him whole, at least a million. It took the prosecutor over a year before giving up on charging Razor for murder. But the lawyer got his satisfaction when they gave Razor an eleven-year sentence. At first, Razor thought about the money and maybe it wouldn't be so bad, then prison life started eating at him. *Yea, I have a plan*, he thought. *I'm going to make you pay, Bull, the same as me only worse. I know how you operate—you'll find a way to get the money in that envelope back and I'll end up with a bullet hole in my head.*

Razor, now forty-two, had worked seven years for Bull on the venture-capital side of his business. He turned a blind eye to Bull's other dealings. Razor had done time off and on before but never eleven years. As Bull threw the package to him that day he told Razor that someone had been shot, cops were on the way, and he couldn't risk being questioned along with everyone else in the building. Now, Bull had a new job for him, and Bull promised Razor this would be his last. He would earn enough to go to a Caribbean island if he wanted, or the coast of France, and retire. This job was riskier but also more rewarding—monetarily. So, Razor found himself speeding down the highway with over a million in his pocket heading to his last job and retirement. *And,* a gut bent on revenge.

It was almost nine o'clock when Razor turned into a motel and he and Lenny walked across the street to a café. A sign, Open 24/7, blinked red and yellow over a picture window. After their meal of hamburgers washed down with a bottle of beer, they strolled back to the Pacific Isle motel. Stopping at the car, they each retrieved a small duffel bag containing the last remnants of prison life. Razor paid for the room and they flopped down on the squeaky beds— their first night of freedom.

———

THE SUN SLICED through a crack in the heavy drapes covering the motel's window.

"Hey, Razor. You awake?"

"Now what, Lenny?"

"Nice, huh? No banging bars."

"Yea."

"I forgot how quiet it is, you know, on the outside."

Razor shifted his six-foot frame, rolling over on his back. He twisted so he could see his cell-mate lying on the other bed.

"Yea, but as nice as this is, wait till you see Daytona Beach with the waves of the Atlantic Ocean lapping over pure white sand."

"I'm excited, Razor. If you say Daytona Beach is where we're heading, then I say let's get a move on." Lenny swung his legs over the side of the bed, stood and stretched. Reaching for his jeans he jammed his foot in the pant leg.

"Come on, Lenny, for God's sake. You're not a bum anymore. Take a shower, and then get dressed. You want to present a new clean-cut image from here on—not some reject from the prison yard. We'll grab some breakfast before hitting the highway."

Lenny chuckled. Razor was right. He was always right. When he heard that he and Razor were being released at the same time he was giddy with the prospect of hooking up with him. Yah, it felt good to be out of prison. He hopped in the shower and washed the grime from the past year down the drain.

While Lenny showered and dressed, Razor brought in the suitcase Bull had packed for him. He told Lenny to go on over to the café. He'd join him after he finished cleaning up.

Razor relished the steamy shower, letting the hot water sluice over his toned body. Taking a look in the mirror he was glad he had stuck to his workout regimen. Other than his milky pallor, nobody would suspect he was an ex-con. He ran his fingers over the trouser's soft fabric as he buttoned, then tucked in the white silk shirt. The black leather belt was as soft as the leather shoes—just as Bull had promised. Razor was surprised to find a gold-chain necklace in the pocket of the suitcase.

Donning a pair of sunglasses, he took a last look in the mirror. He liked what he saw. His black hair needed a trim and he'd have one of those Florida spas shave off his beard, but other than that he was ready for Daytona Beach. The woman he'd corresponded with on FaceBook would have a hard time resisting him. Heck, maybe she would give in to his charms right away.

Chapter 3

Daytona Beach, Florida

JOE ROCKWELL, STOCKBROKER and financial advisor extraordinaire, was throwing a party for his biggest clients. He was known as *Rocket* because he continually raised the worth of the assets under his control. For the past three years, he had avoided the pitfalls of a falling market, a falling dollar, and bank failures when most 401K investments were cut in half. Tonight's cocktail party was to honor the investors who had remained with him through those turbulent years.

Polly Pringle was one of those clients. Her husband had invested their savings with Rocket until the day he died. Polly saw no reason to make a change, and in fact thought Rocket was debonair and enjoyed her appointments with him immensely. She watched a few financial TV shows and always came with a list of questions about this and that stock.

Polly had retrieved her silver-gray flapper dress, that was what her late husband Harold had dubbed it, from a storage bag for the occasion. The sleeveless silk shift hit just below her knees with a pleated flounce. The straight lines of the dress covered the extra pounds she continued to battle, but most thought of her as slim and attractive. The scoop neck was a nice backdrop for her long, multi-strand, pearl necklace, another gift from Harold to wear with the outfit. Her low-heel, strappy silver shoes completed the costume. The June evening air was a balmy seventy-five degrees, normal for this time of year in Daytona Beach. Nonetheless, she draped a geranium-red, cashmere scarf around her shoulders.

Polly entered the opulent lobby of the Rockwell Financial Management building. A small fountain surrounded with greenery served as the focal point of the large space. The trickling water muffled the conversations of the clients waiting their turn to meet with Rocket.

But tonight, the couches were pushed back to the window walls, exposing the velvety, dark-green carpet. Trees tucked between couches were adorned with tiny white lights giving a festive backdrop for three musicians – piano, harp and violin – playing soft chamber music. Buffet tables were laden with hors d'oeuvres and pastries. Shrimp from the gulf and lobster bites from Maine circled small ice sculptures of fish rising from the center of ice-chip beds. Three large vases of flowers—red roses, yellow daisies and spikes of blue gladiolas—adorned teak console tables. Four-foot mirrors behind each bouquet doubled the number of flowers. Pots of lilies perfumed the air.

Rocket spotted Polly as she entered and strode up to greet her.

"Polly, you look beautiful," he said, threading her arm through his, patting her hand.

"Thank you, Rocket. You certainly have a crowd and from the looks of them, the crème de la crème of Daytona Beach society."

"It's been a good year, Polly, and I think we all feel like celebrating. How about a glass of champagne?"

"Well, I certainly can have one, don't you think?"

"Polly, the night calls for at least two."

A smiling, young, auburn-haired waitress, black skirt, white blouse and black spiked heels, approached with a silver tray of champagne flutes. Rocket picked up a flute, handing it to Polly.

Another woman approached, Rocket, smiling broadly, greeted her with a discreet kiss on the cheek.

"Elizabeth, it's great to see you, and I think I've seen that little black dress before."

Liz smiled in agreement.

"I wasn't sure you'd be back from Ocala in time," Rocket said. "Here, I have someone I'd like you to meet. This is Polly Pringle, one of my favorite clients. Polly, meet Elizabeth Stitchway."

The two women shook hands and Rocket whispered to Polly, "Elizabeth is a private investigator in case you ever need help solving a murder."

"Oh my, that is good to know," Polly whispered back.

Another waitress strolled by and Liz helped herself to a glass of champagne.

"You know, Miss Stitchway, if you don't mind, could I chat with you a minute?" Polly asked. "Maybe sit on that couch over there?"

"Of course, Mrs. Pringle."

"Oh, please, call me Polly."

"Polly it is. Why don't you have a seat and I'll fix us a plate of those scrumptious looking goodies while we talk."

"That would be lovely, dear."

Liz returned quickly, setting a small plate of appetizers on the coffee table, and turned to Polly waiting for her to speak.

Polly took a sip of her champagne, smoothed her dress, and then looked at Liz. "When that nice Mr. Rockwell said you were a private investigator, I immediately started thinking about my potential situation," Polly said, helping herself to a toothpick-speared scallop wrapped in bacon.

"A potential situation?"

"Yes, nothing's happened as yet. Tell me, Miss Stitchway—"

"It's Liz."

"Liz, do you work on a confidential basis?"

"My lips are sealed. Anything you tell me goes no further. I promise you that."

"Very well. You see I've been a widow for three years now. I love to go to the symphony and maybe a dinner out. But, Liz, I haven't found an eligible man to fill the bill as my escort." Polly paused taking another sip of champagne. "I've been thinking about joining one of those personal sites—for companionship, mind you. No frolicking about in the bedroom."

"It could be fun, Polly. But you do have to be careful."

"Oh dear, do you think I'm too old?"

"Not at all. You're a beautiful, vibrant woman. Any man would be lucky to act as your escort," Liz replied, smiling confidently at Polly. "But there are a few things you should be aware of when you sign up."

"Well, I've heard of FaceBook but—"

"Oh, I don't think you want to use FaceBook to find a potential escort. People use their real identity—name, picture, that sort of thing on that site. They want to be found by old high school friends, business colleagues who have lost touch, and to make new friends. But the dating thing—you want to protect your identity. Use an alias. Do you have a website in mind?"

Polly looked down at her cocktail napkin and then up at Liz. She giggled nervously. "Yes, I have. Latch dot com—"

"Do you mean Match dot com," Liz interrupted smiling. "Although your version would be a good name for a dating site."

"Yes, yes. I'm a little nervous talking about it I guess. There were several men in my age category—sixty-nine to seventy-three. Does that sound about right to you?"

"I think so. You look much younger than seventy-three."

"Thank you. Seventy-two actually—I thought I'd leave a little leeway," she added smiling. But talking to you just now, what I'd like to know, do you investigate other things or only murder?"

"Fortunately, I guess, there aren't enough murders to keep me busy, and the police handle most of those investigations," Liz said, taking a sip of her champagne enjoying the banter with Polly.

"That's good ... that there aren't that many murders. So, I thought maybe if I got to know someone through email ... well, could you investigate him to be sure he's reputable? I would give you whatever you suggest as a retainer."

"I'm sure we can work something out, and I think it would be fun to play cupid for you. There are a couple of tips I'd like you to keep in mind. When you open an account on a site use an alias. I joined a dating site once but then had to drop out because of an investigation."

"Polly, I thought I might see you here." A woman in a soft, blue-silk A-line dress had walked up to them. Liz noticed her shoes—metallic high heels with rhinestones.

"Liz, I'd like you to meet my neighbor, Victoria Brookfield. Vicky, this is Elizabeth Stitchway. She's a friend of Rocket's."

Liz stood up to shake Vicky's hand just as a man approached, putting his hand against Vicky's back.

"Harri, nice to see you," Polly said. "This is Elizabeth Stitchway. Liz, Harrison Brookfield."

Harri put his glass on the table to shake Liz's hand. Liz noticed Vicky pull away from her husband. He let his hand drop.

I never would have paired these two, Liz thought. *Victoria seems so sophisticated, and Harri, well, he looks out of place with that ponytail, golf shirt and—*

"Nice to meet you, Miss Stitchway."

"Excuse me," Vicky said. "I think I'll refresh my drink."

"Me, too," Harri said. "Catch you later, Polly." He turned to walk with his wife but she had disappeared in the crowd.

Liz sat down again on the couch beside Polly. "*Oh, Oh. Looks like trouble between those two.* "That's a beautiful diamond clip in Vicky's hair," Liz said.

"Yes. Not sure how she can afford it."

"Now, where were we?" Liz asked.

"You were going to give me some advice about finding an escort," Polly whispered.

"Oh, yes. Give yourself a quirky name to start with, and never include anything on the site that identifies who you are, where you live, or your telephone number. All of that is *very* privileged information and not to be given to just anyone. Also, if the messaging within the site gets to a point where you would like to meet the man, you want to be sure the first date is in a very public place, like a cafe for coffee. That's when you size him up."

"It does sound kind of fun, don't you think?" Polly said giggling again.

"It can be as long as you're careful. Now, if you go ahead with your online-dating idea, see if you can get him to tell you his real name. I can check him out. Is that is what you had in mind?"

"That's it exactly. Oh, my dear, we are going to make a great team."

"Well, Polly, I thought that was you."

Polly looked up to see Susan Armstrong standing on the other side of the coffee table with a glass of champagne in her hand staring down at her.

"Hello, Susan. Lovely party isn't it. I didn't know you and your husband were clients of Rocket's."

"For a couple of years. Really, Polly, aren't you going to introduce me to your friend?"

"Of course, excuse my manners. This is Elizabeth Stitchway, and Liz, this is my friend Susan Armstrong."

"You two look like you're cooking up a devilish little scheme. From the buffet table I saw you giggling, Polly. What's up?"

"I was just telling Mrs. Pringle about my dog Maggie—"

"And of course, I had to tell Liz a story about my dear little Regina," Polly quickly added.

"Dogs. Not for me. I'll see you at our quilting-bee, Polly. Nice to meet you, Liz." Susan strutted off for another glass of champagne, her black cocktail dress outlining her slim figure.

"Liz, you are wonderful. Susan is the last person I would want to know about our little arrangement."

"She didn't seem to have a husband with her. Is she married— that was some rock she had on her finger."

"Oh, yes, but I rarely see them together unless it's a big charity event. Now, how do I get in touch with you? A secret phone number?" Polly asked, grinning.

Liz dug in her little black shoulder bag, pulled out her business card, handing it to Polly. "Here are my numbers—office and cell. Are you in the phone book?"

"Yes, and my email address is PPringle@yahoo.com. I have a cell, too. Maybe I should have business cards made up—you know, for my escorts" she said chuckling. "Liz, I saw a write-up in the newspaper about the police department offering a self-defense class for women. There's a class this Monday. What do you think about that?"

"Polly, I think you are going to be a very interesting client. And, a big yes to the self-defense class."

"Oh, good. I'll add it to my finding-an-escort to-do list. Of course, I never thought of hiring my own PI. I'll add you to my list, too."

Liz tilted her head.

"So I can check—done," Polly said lifting her second flute of champagne from the waitress's tray. She tapped her glass to the rim of her private investigator's champagne flute.

The musician's instrumental selection rose over the gathering— Frank Sinatra's, *I'll do it My Way.*

Chapter 4

—

KELLY, SLIDING HER SHOULDER along the wall so as not to bump into anything, padded on bare feet down the hallway to the kitchen in her pink pajamas. She was texting a response to her friend Carol's message about a cute boy Carol met at the library. Pressing the send button she entered the kitchen with a smile and joined her mother. As quick as she sent the message on its way another one popped up in its place.

The mother-daughter pair had a ritual since Kelly was in first grade. Breakfast on Sunday was their time together to discuss what they planned for the upcoming week. Like mother like daughter—both five-and-a-half feet tall, glossy black hair—Vicky's shoulder length, straightened and curved forward framing her face. Kelly's hair tumbled freely in cascading curls to the middle of her back or anchored into a ponytail.

Her father used to eat Sunday breakfast with them, but over the past few years he left early, grabbing coffee and a doughnut on his way to work. Kelly didn't question his working on Sunday as she and her mom enjoyed each other's company. Lately, however, mornings had become frustrating for Vicky. Ever since Kelly had received a hot new smartphone from her mom and dad on her sixteenth birthday, she had become fixated with the device.

Her parents thought the phone was a good idea when they bought the gift, now that Kelly passed the driver's education class receiving her license. In case of an emergency, she could call them for help. But, much to their consternation, she never put it down. They felt they were losing touch with their daughter.

"Kelly, please put that phone away and talk to me. I made your favorite blueberry pancakes. Want me to warm up the syrup? Kelly!"

"What?" Kelly looked up. "Sorry, Mom, what did you say?"

Vicky reached over, gently removing the phone from her daughter's fingers.

"Wait. Wait … okay."

Vicky closed the phone, laid it in the middle of the table and grasped her daughter's empty hand. Leaning forward, she looked into her big violet eyes—under certain lights, sparkling with flecks of blue. It was like looking in a mirror.

"Kelly, I had a call from your science teacher yesterday."

"Why did he call?" Kelly asked furrowing her brows.

"He's worried. You *messed up*, his words, on a multiple-choice exam last week."

"Oh, Mom, he already talked to me about that. I don't know what was the matter with me that day. I knew the answers. It's the first week of summer school and—"

"That's what he thought. He called more out of concern for you than the exam. I guess you're usually very engaged in class, first to raise your hand. But lately, he felt you're withdrawn. He said you moved to the back of the classroom. Why did you change your seat?"

Vicky let go of Kelly's hand and took a sip of her coffee, trying to steady her nerves.

"It was Carol's idea. She wanted me to sit with her," Kelly said looking down at the table.

"Carol's taking the class?"

"Yes. Her parents thought it was a good idea after I signed up. We study together."

"Kelly, school is very important. You want to enroll in pre-med when you graduate from high school next year. You're becoming addicted to your phone, always in immediate contact with your friends. You've suddenly let them run your life. Become your life."

"Mom, I'm not that bad. Carol wanted me to see the messages her latest crush was sending her—"

"You moved to the back of the room to see Carol's messages?"

"I'll move back up front. I will. I promise. Please, don't worry."

"You have a driver's license and the use of a new car. Your dad and I gave you that phone in case of an emergency. If you act responsibly, we'll continue to support you. But, if your grades start to slip, or you abuse what we've given you, we'll take it away. That goes for the car, too."

Vicky stood up and walked to the stove. She had said all she was going to say for the time being. Wiping her hands on the towel sticking out of her jean's back pocket, she picked up the spatula. "How about some pancakes?"

Kelly went to her mother and put her arms around her, snuggling into her familiar warm embrace.

"I'll do better. I promise," Kelly said. "And, I would like some warm syrup." She gave Vicky a squeeze and then stepped to the pantry for the syrup bottle.

"How's the quilt coming along?" Vicky asked. "I saw Polly last night at a party."

"She's so nice and you'll never guess what happened," Kelly said.

"Well, tell me. Get the butter will you, sweetie."

"Polly told us she was thinking about joining a dating site … on the internet."

Vicky looked up sharply from the griddle. "Whatever for?" she asked, staring at the cupboard.

"She wants to find a man who will escort her to the symphony and stuff. And, Susan Armstrong, you know her don't you?"

"Yes, not well though." Vicky regained her composure, setting a platter of four pancakes on the table.

"Mrs. Armstrong dared Mrs. P to join a dating site, and Mildred chimed in and dared her, too."

Vicky, startled at Kelly's words, turned her back to her. Walking to the sink, she stared out the window. Her lips drew up into a small smile. Her secret. Her Facebook pen pal. Maybe, in time, a secret love. However, the secret, that had to remain unfulfilled, warmed her body bringing a flush to her cheeks.

"Mom, I'm going over to Carol's. When do you want me home to help with dinner?"

"Mom?"

"Oh, ah, about three-thirty will be plenty of time."

"I'll be here. What are we having? That leg of lamb in the refrigerator?"

"Yes. Your dad asked, sometime last week, if I would fix lamb."

"I saw the mint jelly when I got the syrup. Sounds like a wonderful dinner. I'm glad Dad's planning on joining us. Mom, is everything going to be alright between you two?"

Vicky turned to her daughter. "Oh, Kelly, don't worry. We've hit a rough patch—"

"Mom, it's more than a patch. It seems forever since you two went out, and, and ... well, kissed."

Vicky's shoulders slumped. She turned back to the window. "We'll work through it, and the three of us are going to have a nice Sunday dinner ... together."

The earlier tension over Kelly's phone, and her questions about her parent's marriage eased. Vicky said she would do the breakfast dishes and shooed Kelly out to get dressed. Because of Kelly's comments on the mint jelly, coupled with Harri's request for a lamb dinner, Vicky decided to make it really special, a family dinner in the dining room. She felt she hadn't been very nice to Harri at Rocket's party last night. They had words in the car about his spending so much time at work. He said, once again, he felt he was close to getting the results he wanted, updating the code on the simulation program. *He really is a good provider,* she mused. She didn't want for anything, but then their needs were modest given the way they had to live.

Vicky checked her menu once again to be sure she had everything for dinner and then set the table in the dining room, complete with candles and crystal wine goblets. After one last check on the timing of the roast, she went up to the bedroom and the book she just purchased at Barnes and Noble—*Letters of Vincent Van Gogh.*

Later in the afternoon, she closed the book and strolled to the kitchen to prepare the leg of lamb for the oven. That done, she showered and changed for dinner in a dress instead of her usual jeans and a white T-shirt.

Kelly came home right on time and peeled the potatoes while Vicky tossed the salad. It was close to five o'clock and Harri still wasn't home. She had suggested to him that maybe a 4:30 cocktail would be nice before dinner. Calling him at the office, he answered the phone on the first ring and promised he'd be home shortly.

———

VICKY AND KELLY ATE in the kitchen. Kelly tried to make light of the situation, but Vicky wasn't having any of it. At eight o'clock Kelly said she was going to go over her science notes and excused herself. Vicky put the food away, loaded the dishwasher, and sat down with a glass of wine. She heard the garage door open and close, and then Harri entered the kitchen. He and his partner had worn business attire in San Francisco, but that had been replaced when he moved to Florida. He stood in his flip-flops, wrinkled cut-offs, and a green T-shirt. He looked at her a moment, tightened the band on his ponytail, and took a step to the table.

"Vicky, I am so sorry. Tom came in, the VP of Engineering—"

"I know who Tom is."

"Yes, well, he wanted me to demonstrate the changes in the simulation … he made a suggestion so, of course, I changed the code so we could see if his idea made any difference and—"

"*Of course*, you did. Harri, did it ever occur to you this afternoon that you had asked me to fix a leg of lamb today … a nice Sunday dinner … the three of us?"

"I said I was sorry."

"That's what you always say, I'm sorry. *Sorry* but we have to leave San Francisco. *Sorry* you have to leave your parents. Oh, yes, and I'm *so sorry* you have to give up your job … it's my career I say, well I truly am *sorry* you have to give up your career." Vicky was on her feet, screaming in Harri's face.

"What do you want me to say? If I'm on the verge of a breakthrough in the code, what do you want me to do?" he yelled back raising his arms, giving up.

"Come home for Sunday dinner. Or, maybe come home for any dinner. That would be a novelty." She yanked open the refrigerator door. "Here, have a piece of lamb. *Sorry* it's a bit cold. Enjoy your dinner."

Vicky poured herself another glass of wine, "And, make yourself comfortable in the study tonight. I'll be reading and I'm *sorry* but I wouldn't want to disturb your sleep with the light in your eyes ... *all night.*"

Chapter 5

Albuquerque, New Mexico

RAZOR DROVE OUT OF California, through Arizona, and into New Mexico. With an early start, two drivers, and eleven hours on the road, it was dinner time. He turned into a desert watering hole near Albuquerque and parked alongside a semi-truck on the dirt lot. He and Lenny climbed out of the vehicle and stretched. Opening the back door, he removed the case containing the laptop computer. It was time to send a couple of messages. He had noticed a dish antenna attached to the side of the weathered building as he approached the bar on the highway. He thought it was worth a try— if not, well, he'd wait until they stopped at a motel for the night. Snapping the car locks down with the key ring, he and Lenny ambled into the bar.

Lenny slid onto a barstool but Razor headed to a table in the back corner next to a staircase. A person stopping by for a bite to eat might think they stumbled into a wild-west movie. Tumbleweeds were snagged by an old wooden fence outside, and inside the wood floors were worn and scratched. One could imagine women prancing down the staircase wrapped in feather boas over scanty costumes to entertain the male patrons.

When Razor didn't sit at the bar, Lenny hustled off to join him at the table in the shadows. The barmaid took their order for two bottles of beer and disappeared. Neither man spoke until after their first swallow of the amber liquid. Lenny squirmed in his chair waiting for Razor to tell him what to do.

Razor, his back to the corner, set up the laptop. Luck was with him—an electrical outlet was on the staircase wall. He could tend to his business without battery power and without anyone looking over his shoulder. Now if he could access the internet life would be sweet.

Razor looked over at Lenny. He was rocking back and forth, fidgeting with his beer bottle, and then sitting on his hands to hold them still. The connection to the internet popped up on the screen.

"Go tell that waitress we'd like something to eat," Razor said, his fingers hovering over the keyboard.

"Sure," Lenny said. "What should we order?"

Scanning the menu, Razor pointed to #6. "That one—Special Enchilada Plate and another beer. You get what you want."

Lenny, eager to please, jumped up with the menu and hustled over to the girl in the short orange skirt.

Razor opened one of his email accounts and sent a message to Bull that the trip was going well. He figured another three days and he'd arrive at his destination. Messages to Bull were never specific, nor in code, in case their accounts were compromised. Razor logged out of email and signed into Facebook, an account for his alias, Richard Stiles. A message was waiting for him from Victoria Brookfield. She said she hadn't heard from him for over a week and hoped all was going well with his business. She signed off, Vicky. Knowing her full name from Bull, she was easy to find on FaceBook. Of course, if she hadn't been on FaceBook, then contacting her would have been more difficult. Bull had done the hard work tracing the phone number and learning where she lived.

Oh, yes, everything is going well, Miss Vicky, he thought. A subtle twisting of his lips—a smile came and went.

The waitress set their orders on the table, along with two more beers. She smiled at Lenny and then returned to the back of the bar. The Arizona Diamondbacks were playing on the television set mounted over the bar and the second baseman had just hit a home run. The fans went wild. A couple of cowboys sitting at the bar gave a fist pump and laughed as they gulped their beers. Lenny dove into his tacos while Razor turned back to his computer and contemplated his reply to Vicky. She was obviously thinking about him. She had sent him a message out of turn—a good sign.

Lenny finished his tacos and took his beer up to the bar to watch the baseball game as well as miss-short-orange skirt.

Razor ate a few bites of his enchilada, took a swig of beer, and then flexed his fingers over the computer keyboard. In Vicky's first message to him, after he had asked her to be a FaceBook friend and after she accepted, she told him she was married and only looking for a pen pal. Their messages had become warmer over his last three months in prison. He told her he was traveling abroad on business and he too was looking for a pen pal. At his gentle nudging, she began to open up to him. She was lonely. Her husband spent most of his waking hours at work.

Bringing up a possible face-to-face meeting with the woman was the next item on Razor's agenda. A meeting ... nothing more than a cup of coffee with a friend ... at first.

> "Dear Vicky, I'm sorry I didn't write sooner. My schedule has been jammed. Your profile says you live in Florida but you didn't include a city. I'm scheduled to be in the Orlando area for several months. Do you live near there? Maybe we could share a cup of coffee? I'd very much like to meet you. Your friend, Richard."

There, he thought. *That might cause her heart to skip a beat. Who knows, maybe settling this last score for Bull will prove to be entertaining ... at least for a little while.*

Smiling, he finished his beer, laid money on the table for the two meals, and signaled Lenny it was time to get going.

Chapter 6

Daytona Beach

SUSAN ARMSTRONG PERUSED HER social calendar and entered the date for the next quilting bee. Satisfied, she hopped into her red convertible to run her housekeeper's errands—groceries, pick up her husband's shirts at the cleaners, and gas in the car. The woman said she came down with the flu and couldn't get out of bed. So, Susan had to take up her slack, all the time wondering if Polly was going to act on the dare the quilters had thrown her way. The thought of chatting with a man online, at a dating site, had given Susan a thrill. In fact, she hadn't felt this excited for a long time.

Her marriage of fifteen years was stale, more than stale. It was defunct. They had no children. Neither one wanted a child. Her husband Charlie had grown distant. He rarely engaged her in conversation, and romance was long gone. The one thing she did enjoy from him was status. He was a prominent attorney in the area, made scads of money, and this, along with her good looks, had catapulted her into the social elite. Before she married Charlie she was a young real estate agent dreaming of selling million-dollar houses. But after meeting Charlie she decided it would be easier to marry the money. Work was not a word in her vocabulary.

I'll be darned if I'm going to sit around without a little fun in my life, she thought. Charlie had stormed out of the house that morning complaining that they were out of coffee. Again. "It must be hard to squeeze a can of coffee on your list of things to do between golf and charity events. Haven't you heard? Charity starts at home," he said sarcastically. The door to the garage slammed shut. A few minutes later she heard his Jeep screech out of the driveway and down the road.

Pouring a glass of white wine, and along with a small bowl of carrot sticks and red-pepper hummus dip, she left the kitchen. At thirty-nine, she was conscious of her shapely figure and worked to keep it that way. Ascending the spiral staircase from the foyer with a spring in her step, she eagerly walked down the hall with blue-silk damask walls over creamy white wainscoting. She turned into her sitting room and settled in front of her computer. The room spelled female—pale-pink walls, white woodwork, lace curtains gathered across a picture window, a white fan trimmed in gold providing a soft breeze.

While the computer was starting up, Susan went to her closet and retrieved a small box from the top shelf. Opening the box she carefully picked up the blonde wig and turned to face the closet mirror. Putting on the wig, she tucked her chestnut-brown hair underneath the wig's soft curls. Satisfied with the transformation, she returned to her computer.

She was sure if she registered at a site it would request an e-mail address. Not wanting anyone to know what she was doing, she created a new account on Yahoo, nasus39—her name backwards and her age. That done, she performed a Google search for *online dating*.

"Wow, 49-million." Nibbling on a carrot stick, she read through the first two pages of results which, after the initial listings, were general sites—anything to do with dating. She recognized two of the first three—eHarmony and Match.com. The first on the list, Zoosk, was new to her but stated it was free to join. OkCupid was also free. The others had membership payment plans depending on how many months you wanted to try to meet the man or woman of your dreams.

Deciding on Match.com, she clicked on the link. There was no join button just two checkboxes: choose your sex and their sex. *Pretty easy*, she thought. She clicked Woman seeking a Man. Continue. Typed her zip code. Continue. Username? *Umm, how about Rainbow?* Continue. Password. She entered her birth date. Continue.

After a few more screens she was able to do a preliminary search. Setting the criteria to, Man, age 38 to 50, within 40 miles of the zip code, she then clicked on search. A listing of 1101 men popped onto her screen.

"Oh my, Polly. You are in for a treat. Just look at these handsome guys. Of course, your results will be vastly different than mine ... old geezers." Sipping her wine, she pondered for a second on whether to subscribe or not. "What the heck. Can't hurt anything, and I'm not Susan with brown hair, I'm Rainbow, a blonde. I'll stop at one of those picture-taking booths down on the beach and get a photo of the new me that I can post to my profile. Rainbow's profile." She clicked "Subscribe" and began to fill-in the requested information.

She picked the easy questions first: height, hair and eye color, slender body type. She paused on relationship status. "Well, if I'm going to chat with someone I guess I should pick divorced. Of course, I could say separated. I'll come back to that later." She clicked save.

Standing up, Susan stretched and sauntered downstairs to the kitchen to add more wine to her glass. Standing at her kitchen window, her eyes followed two squirrels chasing each other, round and round the tree. She switched her gaze to the bird bath where a robin was splashing. *Animals are lucky. No tricky relationships,* she thought. "Might as well finish up with the subscription. It'll be time for dinner soon—a plate for me and a plate in the refrigerator for Charlie. I'll be eating alone ... again." She sighed and returned upstairs to her computer.

The first thing she did was click the subscribe button, picked the three-month payment plan, and then continued with the questionnaire. There were several questions to be filled out with 260 words or less slowing her down: how do you spend your free time, favorite places and things. Smoker—no way. Children—none. How tall should he be? "Hmm ... I like a tall man, maybe six foot to six-foot-four."

Then the questions became specific on the man she was looking for—what he should look like, hair and eye color. Then she was stumped—describe yourself and your ideal match. She clicked "Save" and shut down her computer.

Susan finished her wine and decided a nice hot bath in the Jacuzzi tub would be just the ticket while she thought about her answers to the questions she'd skipped. The tub filled and she added bubble bath to the water. Stepping into the warm water, she submerged herself in the bubbles and closed her eyes.

"Maybe I *will* rendezvous with him *if* he sounds nice. As long as I'm discreet, how could it hurt?"

Chapter 7

———

BALMY AIR DRIFTED IN the car window as Polly drove herself and Mildred on their merry way to the women-only, self-defense class at the Port Orange Police Department. Polly, dressed in a new black Nike jogging suit, turned the car into the parking lot.

"I'm a little nervous. How about you," Mildred asked.

"A little. Cute jogging suit. New?" Polly asked sliding out of the car.

"Yes," Mildred replied, joining Polly on the other side of the car. "I thought if I was going to practice being mugged I'd look good. The blue matches my eyes don't you think?" Mildred turned to Polly, fluttering her lashes.

"Definitely a match," Polly smiled.

"I wonder if we'll know anybody?"

"The class is limited to twenty women, so I doubt it," Polly replied.

Within minutes they were checking in with a woman sitting behind a plate-glass window. She handed them a white stick-on name tag and instructed Polly and Mildred to go down the hall and take the first door on their left.

Light-yellow paint on the walls softened the atmosphere but didn't hide the fact they were in a fortified, cement-block building. Walking through a scanner, similar to what they had experienced at an airport, they entered the classroom.

Polly guided Mildred to the center of the first row of seats. The room was set up with rows of seven-foot folding tables—two chairs positioned behind each table. A few attendees were talking quietly and very quickly the remainder of the class was seated. A tall, head shaved bald, man dressed in a gray-cotton jogging suit, and the physique of a prize fighter, entered. He introduced himself as Detective Jim Miles. He began handing out booklets to each woman, smiling and chatting as he made his way around the room.

"I'm glad to see we have a full class," Detective Miles said walking back to the front of the class. "The pamphlet I just handed you contains an overview of what you will hear, see, and do over the next two hours. First, I'm going to show you a ten-minute film. The balance of the time will be spent in the gym where you'll learn, and practice, how to defend yourself in case you're attacked."

Detective Miles paused, looking around with intense blue eyes at the ladies sitting in front of him. "Any of you ever been attacked?"

Two women, sitting at different tables, raised their hands—one a bit timid but the other, a petite, middle-aged woman, shot her hand up in the air and then stood up.

"Well, I'm glad to see you beat up the creep, Betty. It's Betty isn't it?"

A few chuckles could be heard as the students looked at the woman who was standing.

"Yes, sir," Betty said, smoothing the sleeves of her red jogging suit.

"What did you do?" Miles asked.

"Screamed bloody murder," Betty blurted out. "About broke my eardrums."

"And, Betty, what did your assailant do?"

"He ran like the devil … away from me."

"Ah, you surprised him. He didn't want to tangle with you. Good job."

A young lady on the end of the third row, her blonde ponytail flipping in the air, waved her hand to get his attention. "I'd be so afraid if someone came after me. I'm sure I'd just stand there like a dummy."

"Fear is your normal instinct. Fear kicks in and you freeze. Hopefully, by the time you try a few moves in the gym, you'll learn how to tamp down that instinct and replace it with anger and fight, like Betty did."

The detective dimmed the lights, started the film, and then stood to the side of the room, leaning against the wall.

"How about those muscles bulging under that T-shirt, Mildred? I certainly wouldn't mind having him as an escort," Polly whispered.

Polly and Mildred sat straight in their chairs watching the film as woman after woman thwarted her attacker. Between each attack the narrator explained the moves the woman used to escape her situation. As the film came to a close, Detective Miles snapped on the lights.

"Okay, what's the first thing you saw each woman do when she found herself under attack?"

Polly spoke up. "They all said, no."

"No, Polly. They didn't say no. They screamed, NO! And, they screamed, NO, not once, but kept screaming it. NO! NO! NO!" Miles hollered. "And, they continued to yell, NO. Yelling NO, if you take away nothing else from this class, will help replace your fear instinct. You're warning your assailant that *you* are going to fight. What else did they do as they screamed, NO?" Each time Miles said the word no, his voice boomed louder.

A teenage girl in the back called out. "They put up their dukes."

Miles laughed along with others. "That's right," he said. "Only we'll call it moving into a defensive stance. You're giving a clear signal that he'd better back off—like Betty did. What else did you notice?"

Mildred spoke up in a timid voice. "Well, most, maybe all were shoved to the ground and they kicked hard with their feet. They probably hurt the poor guy."

"Ah, Mildred, you felt sorry for the guy?"

"A little I guess."

"Class, this is the second important thing to remember. NEVER NEVER feel sorry for someone who is trying to hurt you. NEVER! How dare he even think of harming you. THE BASTARD! HOW DARE HE think so little of you. You're not going to feel sorry for the bastard. You're going to make sure he doesn't get up off the ground," Miles said looking into the eyes of his students, commanding eye contact from each.

"What about mace? Can I blast him in the face with it?" an Asian woman on the left side of the room asked.

"Sure you can," Miles answered, striding over to her. "But usually an attack is sudden. You don't have time to pull that little mace sprayer out of your purse. If you can, great. But what you'll learn here is how to use the tools that are readily available to you. Your arms, legs, feet, and, most important, your voice yelling NO!" The officer's voice boomed out again. The word "NO" bouncing off the walls.

Miles walked to the other side of the room, opened a door, and motioned the ladies to follow him into the gym. A dark-blue, foam-filled mat, about ten-by-ten feet square, was lying on the highly-polished, wooden floor in the center of the gym.

"Please, form a circle around me," Miles instructed.

The women shuffled around. Bits of nervous conversation were shared by some.

"I'm going to show you different approaches your assailant might use to attack you and then how you can retaliate to stop him. Of course, the first thing you do is?" He waited. He waited. Then a few women said in unison, "You say, no."

"Wrong," Miles replied. "You yell, NO. What is it you're going to do?"

"NO," they shouted

"SCREAM IT OUT," Miles yelled.

All twenty screamed at the top of their lungs, "NO."

"AGAIN," Miles yelled.

"NO!"

"That's better," he whispered.

Miles had donned several padded devices for protection. Then over the next thirty minutes he demonstrated various attacks, each with a different student playing the victim and how she could thwart her assailant. Each woman screamed, "NO," as Miles moved in to attack. They followed up with different body moves he demonstrated including kneeing and kicking a man where it would hurt.

"Now, if your assailant comes at you from behind ... Polly, please come here so we can demonstrate."

Polly walked to the center of the mat as Miles instructed, and he circled in back of her explaining what he was going to do. "The attacker will come up from behind and put his arms around you, probably your rib cage. He is more than likely going to be taller than you so, as he encircles you, he will bend forward—over you." As Miles talked he lightly put his arms around Polly's rib cage. Looking at the class, he said, "Your defensive move is to scream, NO, and at the same time plant your feet and give him a good headbutt with the back of your head—hit his nose hard. Remember, he's doubtless taller than you and bending over so his nose will be the target. Okay, slow at first, Polly. He puts his arms around you, you plant your feet, scream, NO, and flip your head back hard."

Polly didn't hear the slow part. When he said scream and flip your head back hard she did so, surprising Detective Miles who instinctively tightened his arms as her head came back at his nose. A pop was heard by everyone in the room.

"Polly, was that your rib? Are you okay," Miles asked turning her around.

"Yes, it was. It happens … pops. I'm fine, really," she said smiling.

"Are you sure?" Miles asked. "I'm always very careful in this class. I've never broken a woman's rib."

Miles demonstrated another move with a different student, and then the class ended. The women filed out of the gym, chatting and laughing.

"Did you see that? She hit him bang in his snot-locker," Betty said. Those within earshot laughed again, picked up their belongings in the classroom and left the building.

"Miles called out to Polly as she and Mildred headed to the door. "Are you sure you're okay, Polly?"

"Yes, thanks. Great class."

Out in the car, Mildred looked at her friend. "Polly, your rib must hurt. Everyone heard it snap."

"It will definitely smart tomorrow … probably for several weeks. I just didn't have the heart to tell Detectives Miles."

Chapter 8

Houston, Texas

RAZOR AND LENNY WHIZZED by the sign: "Welcome to the State of Texas." They were both singing the Johnny Cash song, *I Walk The Line*, at the top of their lungs. Razor kept beat pounding the steering wheel. Lenny rolled down the window and slapped the outside of his door in cadence with Razor. The two sang the song again, laughed and then fell silent. Lenny stuck his head out the window, took a deep breath. *Ah, sweet freedom,* he thought.

Pulling himself back inside the car, he looked over at Razor. "You sure do know how to pick'em—your friends. This car is like a grizzly bear with a nose hot on the honey trail."

Razor didn't pay any attention to his companion. He was actually thinking of ditching him along the way. He wanted to help the kid go straight, but he seemed scattered brained, if there was even a brain in his head. Maybe he couldn't hold a job.

"How far do you figure we'll drive today?" Lenny asked.

"What?"

"I said, how far we gonna drive today?"

"I'd like to get through Houston. It'll be a long day, about fourteen hours. Longer tomorrow, fifteen hours give or take. That'll put us in Daytona Beach in four days. With two of us we could have driven straight through, but there's no need to kill ourselves. Four days will be good enough."

Lenny scrunched down in his seat, pulled his ball cap down over his blonde curls, and shut his eyes. Within minutes his mouth dropped open and steady breathing turned into a soft snore.

Razor, happy to trade his companion's yammering for snoring, thought about what he was going to do once he hooked up with his old pal Billy. He'd crash with him for a day or two until he found a condo to rent. The snowbirds would have headed north so he thought he should be able to find something on the ocean, or the Halifax River, at a reasonable rate. He wanted something classy. Get in the proper frame of mind for retirement—trading cement-block walls for a balcony overlooking the water, a martini in his hand with big stuffed olives, or maybe those little cocktail onions. Preparing for this job, he'd done a lot of research the last few months in prison where he had access a few hours a day to a computer and the internet. Seemed like a great way to meet women, wealthy women. But women were not part of his plan, at least not yet. Only one woman had his attention. His complete attention.

The miles swept by.

"Lenny. Lenny, wake up." Razor shook Lenny's arm.

"Yea. Yea. I'm awake." Lenny slowly sat up straight, rubbing his eyes. "What's up?"

"Ever see Houston?"

"No, never. Ooooh … look at those roads zigzagging over each other. I never seen nothing like that. All them roads. Makes me dizzy."

"It's getting dark … not much traffic so we'll breeze through the city. Anyway we'll be close enough."

"Close enough to what, Razor?"

Chapter 9

———

ON THE ROAD AGAIN after several hours sleep, Razor's mind was playing tricks on him. He could swear the salt air from the ocean was blowing in his car window. The Atlantic was still miles ahead, but he was closing in on his destination at eighty-five-miles-per hour. Lenny was getting on his nerves. Both were anxious to put an end to the trip.

Daydreaming about his plan—getting a place to stay without a cellmate—was Razor's first priority. *I think I'll treat myself to a few hours at a spa—a pretty lady massaging the kinks from my back after four days of travel. I bet someone there could style my hair, and oh, yea, a shave with some of those sweet-smelling oils.* He smiled. *After all, I want to be a gentleman ready to fill Victoria's lonely life. Lure her into my trap.*

The sign over I-95 indicated St. Augustine was three miles ahead and a rest area in five. *Perfect. I'll stop, grab a cup of coffee, and give Billy a call.*

"Hey, Lenny."

"What. What." Lenny sat up, shook his head. "Are we there? Wow. Look at them palm trees."

"No, but I'm stopping. I have to call Billy and let him know we're only a couple of hours away. Grab yourself a snack."

Razor pulled under the shade of a stand of stately palms. After a quick trip to the restroom, and buying a cup of coffee from a pretty attendant, he walked outside to a bench and placed a call to Billy.

The phone was picked up on the third ring. "Who's this?"

"Billy, it's me, Razor."

"Shit, where have you been? I've been waiting for your call."

"I should have buzzed you when we left Houston but it was two in the morning."

Billy chuckled. "Glad you didn't. Two in the morning?"

"Yea, but the end's in sight. I'm tired of being on the road. Lenny and I are just outside of St. Augustine so we should be at your place in a little while. You still in the same mobile park?"

"Yah. (replace "Yah" with "Yep") Who's Lenny?"

"Hold on a minute."

A station wagon parked next to Razor's SUV and five squealing kids barreled out in all directions. They were obviously happy to be free of the confines of their car.

"I can't hear you?" Billy yelled into the phone.

"I said to wait a minute. A bunch of kids just disembarked a stuffy ark."

"What the heck are you talking about? Answer me. Who's Lenny?"

"Keep your britches on. He's a friend of mine ... sort of. He needs a job. Do you think you can hook him up with a lawn crew until he finds something he likes?"

"Maybe. I'm planting some bushes at one of my customer's now. She lives one house away from your target," Billy said. "When you get to my place go on in—the door isn't locked. Help yourself to whatever you want. I should be there within an hour after you settle in. I can't wait to see your sorry face."

Chapter 10

—

IT WAS FOUR O'CLOCK in the afternoon, time for the quilters to arrive. Polly had received a request from the Quilts of Valor organization asking for their quilt as soon as possible, so she called the group together for a mid-week session. Kelly's summer class met in the morning so late afternoon proved to be the only time everyone could gather.

Mildred pulled her lace curtain aside to see if Susan's car was parked in front of Polly's house. Billy, Polly's gardener was planting an azalea bush in her front yard. He stopped digging and reached in his pocket retrieving his cell phone. Mildred saw him grin, put the phone back in his pocket, and continue with the azalea. She drew back a little from her window. She didn't trust Billy. His gray hair always looked unkempt, hanging from under his ball cap brushing his shoulders. His jeans looked as soiled as his beat-up red truck. Of course, his job required working in the dirt. Mildred wished she was inside Polly's house so she didn't have to walk in front of him.

Letting the curtain fall back into place, she briskly walked to the back door and locked it. Next, she checked the windows in her bedroom to be sure they were bolted, and then hurried to the front door and stepped out. Dressed in a fresh flowered house dress, this time with a pink apron, she locked the door with a flourish and looked around at Billy just as Susan drove up parking in Polly's driveway. Mildred bustled up the sidewalk to greet her.

Kelly and her mother emerged from their front door, ran across the lawn to Polly's house, slipping in the front door on Susan's heels.

"Hi, Polly. Mom wants to see the quilt we're working on."

"Vicky, come on in the dining room. We think it's going to be a masterpiece," Polly said smiling. "Kelly, what's that on your wrist?"

"It's a brace. I only have to—"

"I know what it is—carpal tunnel," Susan said. "That phone of yours and all that text messaging. I read about it in the doctor's office. Repetitive stress."

"That's right, Susan," Vicky said.

"I'm supposed to take breaks and swap my texting with something else. I'm trying the breaks first. Replacing the texting is proving harder," Kelly said. "I'm just glad it's my left hand, although the brace isn't bothering me too much. After the shot, the pain almost went away."

"The doctor gave her an anti-inflammatory shot, cortisone, and the brace. If she'll just let up on the texting, he thinks the wrist will return to normal in a few weeks," Vicky said.

"But, in the meantime, I can take pictures. No problem. Everyone, group hug," Kelly said, holding up her cell. "Mildred, squeeze in a little closer. Perfect."

Vicky admired the quilt and then excused herself. Kelly gave her mom a hug as she left the house and then returned to her spot at the table.

"Hello, Mrs. Brookfield," Billy called out. Standing up, he brushed the dirt from his knees and approached her.

"Hi, Billy. That's a beautiful pink flowering shrub you just planted."

"I could take good care of your garden, too. I like to have several gardens to tend in the same neighborhood. Cuts down on the driving," he replied grinning.

"Afraid not, Billy. My husband tends to our yard. At least he says that's what he's going to do ... maybe one of these days."

"Well, just let me know next time I'm here at Mrs. Pringle's. That Hawthorn bush is covering your windows on this side of the house. Bet you can't even see out."

Vicky wrapped her arms around herself and walked to the side of her house. "You're right. I hadn't noticed." She smiled briefly without looking at Billy, turned, and ambled back into the house.

———

POLLY HAD LAID THE quilt over the table and each woman sat down in front of her section. Kelly closed her phone and took her seat. She threaded her needle with light-blue thread to work on the matching patches making up her section. The colorful threads were forming a unique pattern on the light-blue underside of the quilt.

"How's your rib today, Polly," Mildred asked.

"Rib? What's the matter with your rib," Susan quipped, pulling her needle with yellow thread through the fabric.

"You missed a good one, Susan," Mildred said. "Our friend Polly had her rib cracked by a very handsome police officer. A detective. Didn't you, Polly?"

"Sorry you couldn't join us, Susan," Polly said. "The class was very interesting and we learned to yell."

"Never mind the yelling. What about your rib?" Susan said.

"This officer, Detective Miles—"

"The very muscular Detective Miles," Mildred giggled.

Maybe I should have gone. I think I'll check when the next class is scheduled, Susan thought, her eyes not wavering from Polly.

"Well, as I was saying, the officer asked me to help illustrate what to do if I was attacked from behind. I guess I was a little too quick for him because he tightened his grip around my rib cage to protect himself. That's when my rib popped."

"The whole class heard it. Too bad he wasn't older, Polly. You could ask him to escort you to the symphony," Mildred said looking at Polly over her glasses.

Susan walked to the buffet and poured a cup of coffee, added cream and sugar and strolled back to her chair taking a sip before setting the cup on the small table behind her. Hearing a quack, quack, she turned to Kelly. "You're friend Carol?"

"Afraid so," Kelly said, fishing her phone out of her shirt pocket and at the same time jumping up out of chair, slamming into Susan. Coffee flew everywhere.

"Oh, Susan, I'm so sorry. Carol, I'll call you back."

Polly ran to the kitchen, soaked a dishtowel with water, grabbed a roll of paper toweling, skittering back to the dining room. Susan was trying to wipe coffee from her blouse with her hand. She grabbed the wet dishtowel from Polly and hightailed it back to the kitchen to add more water to the towel. Mildred took the roll of paper towel from Polly's other hand and wiped down the back of her chair.

"You'd better put some water on those spots where the coffee hit the quilt. Do you have any of that spot cleaner," Mildred asked.

"Yes, I'll get it," Polly replied, hurrying from the room.

Kelly punched in Carol's number and walked with her head down toward the front door. Not realizing it was standing open, she walked smack into it, crying out in pain and dropping her phone.

"Oh dear." Polly ran to her young friend. "Here let me see." Polly gently pulled Kelly's hands from her face. "Mildred, bring that paper towel. Kelly has a nosebleed, and oh my, your forehead is already sporting a goose egg. You're going to have a black and blue ... ouch," Polly exclaimed pulling back. Kelly had raised her hand to feel her forehead and accidentally hit Polly's cracked rib with her brace.

———

POLLY WAVED TO HER friends as they left—Kelly holding a package of frozen peas to her forehead, Susan's blouse clinging to her body still dripping from the soaking in the kitchen sink, and Mildred scurrying down her walkway, head down, avoiding Billy's glance.

Polly closed the door, leaned back against it, and replayed the melee that had transpired in her dining room. "Thank goodness that's over," she said. "Nothing happened that can't be fixed."

She ambled into her sunny, yellow kitchen and put the water on to heat for a cup of tea. Waiting for the water to boil, she sauntered to her work room and turned on her computer. Returning to the kitchen, she fixed her Earl Gray tea, squeezed a slice of lemon over the cup, and walked back to her computer.

"Time to check out a couple of those dating sites."

Chapter 11

—

POLLY'S HEART SKIPPED A BEAT. Having signed up three days ago on SeniorFriendFinder, she certainly was a senior, she was now looking at two messages in her personal mailbox on the website.

Polly clicked to open message 1.

> "11:23 am, *beachnick* wrote:
>
> Hi pretty lady. I do hope you are well. I hadn't noticed your profile before. If you would like to chat send me a message. I'm a widower, too. P.S. you have a lovely smile ... John."

"That's a nice little message," Polly murmured. Clicking on message 2, she took a taste of her strawberry yogurt waiting for the text to display on the screen.

> "2:45 pm, *jets734* wrote:
>
> Hi friend2chat. Nice handle. Just saw your profile. Take a look at mine and if you want to know more send me a message. Sam."

Polly sat back, eyes wide, lips forming a sly smile. *This is fun,* she thought. *Not enough information to give Elizabeth to check.* "Let's see ... what should I say? I don't want to appear too eager. I know." Opening John's message, she typed a couple of sentences thanking him for writing and, yes, she would like to chat. She told him she was going out to work in her garden and hoped he would have a nice day. "I guess that's enough for you, John," she said as she hit the send button.

She opened Sam's message and typed a reply.

> "3:12 pm, friend2chat wrote:
>
> Hi Sam,
>
> My handle, as you say, makes me sound like a trucker. Nice to meet you on the friendship highway. Hope you're having a nice day. I'm on way out the door with my dear little Regina, a Shih Tzu rescue dog. She's going to help me spread some mulch. Polly."

She clicked the computer's turn-off button and walked to her bedroom to change into gardening overalls.

An hour later, sweaty from spreading mulch around the new azalea bed that Billy had planted, she took a shower, put on a pair of tan capris under a black T, and then popped a frozen pizza in the 450-degree oven for dinner. Setting the timer, she felt a tug from her computer. With a glass of Merlot in hand, she watched the screen flit around with the start-up routine and wondered if she would find any new messages in her inbox.

She was not disappointed. John had replied. He said that he looked at her profile again, and her smile had urged him to write to her.

> "3:42 pm, *beachnick* wrote:
>
> "We live in the same city so how about we meet for coffee or better yet, dinner. You say in your profile that you like the beach so let's rendezvous at the Afterdeck. We could send messages back and forth for days, but until you meet someone face-to-face you really don't know if the chemistry is there. Tomorrow evening, 7 o'clock? John Clark."

> "5:38 pm, friend2chat wrote:
>
> Hi John, I suppose dinner would be nice—but I pay for my own. Tomorrow it is, seven o'clock, at the Afterdeck. Polly."

Polly felt like a school girl dressing for her first date. The Afterdeck was a very casual restaurant on the beach, even rowdy at times with a few pop musicians singing as they strummed their guitars and beat their drums. Looking in her closet for what to wear, she decided on her white capris, with a black print-on-white rayon top. *My black jeweled sandals will be nice*, she thought as she laid the outfit on the bed. After a shower and dressing, she put on the finishing touches of her makeup.

"Why am I doing this?" she asked the woman in the mirror, her blood racing with excitement and dread. "Friend. You wanted to meet a friend. A male friend. That's why you're doing this. So go. Go."

An hour later Polly walked into the restaurant and told the hostess she was meeting a friend. "Did a gentleman leave his name … John Clark?" she asked.

"Are you Polly?" the hostess replied with a grin.

"Yes, that's me," Polly said with a nervous chuckle. She followed the hostess to the far side of the dining room, glancing at any man sitting alone as she passed, wondering if he was the one. Three musicians had returned to the small raised platform and began belting out a lively rap song.

He would be nice, she thought. But, the hostess whizzed by Mr. Nice.

"John, I found your dinner date."

The hostess stepped aside and Polly gulped. A gray-haired man stood to greet her. He was nothing like what his profile had portrayed—shorter, much shorter, and much older.

Being a lady, she recovered her manners, nodded to the hostess and quickly sat down opposite the man, the little old man.

How am I going to get out of this? she thought.

"Nice to meet you, John," she said forcing her lips into a smile.

"Ah, Polly, your smile is even lovelier in person. You noted in your profile that you were a light social drinker so I took the liberty of ordering a Manhattan for each of us."

"Oh, all right. I usually have wine with dinner, but a Manhattan sounds perfect at the moment."

John turned out to be a talker so Polly only had to nod, saying "really," or "that's nice" or "that's not so nice," as she planned her escape.

Dinner finally came to an end and Polly took out her wallet to lay cash on the tray holding the bill. She was horrified when John, who smiled saying how much he had enjoyed her company, grabbed the check and handed it with his credit card to the waitress who ran in the opposite direction.

After the hostess returned with the completed transaction, Polly said she had to be getting home and thanked John for dinner. But he insisted on walking her to the car. On the way, he again said how much he enjoyed her company and wondered if she would accompany him to Atlanta. His sister and her husband were celebrating their anniversary with a party this Saturday.

"Oh, my. No. I can't. My daughter ... my daughter is coming for a visit tomorrow, a long visit. But I hope you have a nice time. Bye." Polly quickly slid into her car, closed the door, turned the key and shot out of the parking lot.

———

POLLY WALKED SLOWLY into her kitchen, threw her keys on the counter, and let out a deep sigh as she dialed Elizabeth Stitchway. The phone rang three times and then requested the caller to leave a message.

"Hi, Liz. This is Polly Pringle. You know that piece of advice you gave me about always meeting a blind date for coffee the first time? Well, I violated the rule. But believe me, never again. His name was John Clark. Talk to you soon."

Too restless to go to bed, Polly went to her computer to see what was happening in the news. She again was drawn to see if she had received any new messages. But first, she sent John a Dear-John message.

"9:45 pm, friend2chat wrote:

It was lovely to meet you and thank you for dinner. I don't think we have enough in common to meet a second time. Good luck in your search for a companion. Polly."

She clicked send and then checked her mailbox. She had three new messages.

Chapter 12

——

TAKING THE LEAP FROM casual email chit-chat with her friend Richard, who befriended her on FaceBook over the last few months, to actually meeting him in person was a big step for Vicky. She had allowed herself to fantasize him as an unrequited love, but had not forced herself to replace the fantasy with friendship, a pen pal. And so she had rationalized her way back across the big divide.

The house was eerily quiet as Vicky dressed to meet Richard, who she now insisted on thinking of as her pen pal. Her hands shook making it difficult to put on her earrings.

"Friends. Friends. That's all," she whispered to her reflection as she applied mascara to her eyelashes.

"After all, meeting for coffee in the Barnes and Noble bookstore could hardly be seen as something illicit. Illicit. Why did you use that word? Get a grip, Victoria. When you were a marketing manager in San Francisco, you met with lots of men—business meetings, conferences. No problem then! No problem now!"

Feeling calmer, she shot a spritz of Chanel in the air and took one last look at her image. Her pale-blue silky dress skimmed her body to the middle of her knees. Silver, gem encrusted sandals completed her Florida look. "Okay. Let's go."

——

THE LUNCH-TIME BOOK browsers had vacated the café except for one lone woman sipping coffee, her laptop holding her attention at the small table next to a half-wall separating the café from the rows upon rows of bookcases that made up the bookstore's interior. A slight aroma of hazelnut permeated the air.

Vicky ordered a large coffee and looked around deciding where to sit as she waited for her pen pal. A voice from the left called to her.

"Victoria. Victoria. Hi. I'm Richard." A man strolled up to her from the sitting area just outside of the café. Picking up her coffee she turned to greet him. Stunned, she remained rooted to the spot where she stood. It wasn't just his looks, but his size, his demeanor … he presented an overpowering figure. She saw by his expression — a softness around his large, dark-brown eyes, a genuine smile showing he, too, was taken with her.

Recovering, at least a little, she offered her hand. "Hi, nice to meet you. Any problem finding the store? Not too far from Orlando?"

"No, no. Please, come have a seat. I put my briefcase on that little table in the art section." Settling at the table, he sought her eyes. "Your picture doesn't do you justice," he said tapping his Styrofoam cup to hers.

"And, cheers to you." Suddenly the butterflies were gone, the nerves settled. She relaxed enjoying the conversation with this intriguing gentleman. She wanted to know all about him, and began peppering him with questions.

When she asked about his work, he laughed. "I guess you'd call me a business consultant. My clients are from all over — Europe, South America, but mainly the states, west coast, San Francisco, and, of course, Florida.

"San Francisco—that's where I grew up. I graduated from Stanford, worked a few years, and lucked out when the marketing manager at this tech company left. I stepped into the opening. Great timing."

"How did you happen to move to Florida," he asked, swirling the coffee gently in his cup.

"Oh, well … my husband started a new company. He designed a unique computer chip, and … well, a … venture capitalist put up the money."

"But you didn't go back to work?" Richard asked.

His voice was soft. His eyes warm—the butterflies returned. "No, I didn't," she said, looking down at her hands. "I have a beautiful daughter. She turned sixteen a little while ago."

"Does she look like her mother?" Richard asked

"People say so."

"Then she must be beautiful. I sense you don't want to talk about your past. It's okay, Victoria, I—"

"Vicky. You can call me Vicky," she said turning to watch a woman selecting a Monet picture book, then replacing it on the shelf.

"I'd like to call you Victoria if you don't mind. When I saw you standing with your coffee ... looking for me, well, you're a very sophisticated, lovely woman. Victoria suits you. From your messages, I got the impression that you were lonely. Maybe that's why you were reaching out for a friend. I don't mean to pry, but you wrote as if your marriage was in trouble."

"Oh, no." Startled that he had jumped to such a conclusion, the right conclusion, she looked at him shaking her head. Panicked. "Just normal stresses, ups and downs—all marriages go through them."

He reached into his oversized briefcase—large in width and length, but not too thick. Pulling out a sketchpad and a drawing pencil, he leaned back in the chair studying her.

"I guess it's one of those times ... nice time to have a friend you can talk to," he said.

"Exactly." Her breathing eased back under control. "How about you? Married?"

"No," he said. He tapped the side of her cup with his finger, then looked up at her. Holding the tablet at an angle supported by the table, he began to sketch. "There was a woman once. We thought about it, getting married, but she couldn't take my job."

"Your job?"

He now moved the pencil with long, quick strokes—looking up at her then down at the pad.

"All the traveling. The absences. We both moved on. By the way," he said reaching again into his case. "I bought you a present." He lifted a small package wrapped in pale-blue tissue paper setting it on the table in front of her.

"Oh, Richard, I can't. We just met and—"

"Nonsense. We've been writing to each other for months. I feel like I know you pretty well, but I'd like to get to know you better. Go ahead. Open it."

Victoria picked up the package. Gazed down at it. Hesitating. He watched her holding his gift. She carefully pulled the end of the narrow, white-satin ribbon. The bow fell away. Turning the delicate package over, she slit open the gold sticker and carefully pulled the tissue back. A silk scarf in muted patterns of yellow, blue, and violet beckoned her touch.

"Richard, it's beautiful and blue is my favorite color."

"I'm glad you like it. Drape it around your neck. I'd like to see how it looks on you."

Victoria ran her fingers over the soft silky fabric then loosely let it fall around her neck. Richard sketched again. Slower than before ... the hush of the bookstore enveloping them.

"Your messages saw me through some difficult months. This is my way of saying thank you."

"May I see your drawing?"

"It's not finished—only a sketch. I'll paint it later, but I wanted to capture you ... this moment."

"Do you always carry drawing paper with you?"

"Quite often. I thought I might see something while I waited for you and then you stepped into the picture."

"What if we hadn't ... hadn't enjoyed each other's company?"

"But we do."

Chapter 13

———

HOT, HUMID, SUMMER AIR smothered the east coast of Florida. Razor opened all the car windows letting the breeze flow freely throughout the SUV. Floridians cranked their car air conditioners up high, but to Razor, after the cold, damp prison air, the hot breeze felt like kisses from angels.

Meeting Victoria had been a snap. He left her eating out of his hand. Or, was it the other way around? He admitted to himself he had enjoyed being with her. The scarf was a touch of genius. She seemed genuinely thrilled with his gift. From her reaction, he surmised her husband never gave her anything so personal. Yet, if he was being honest, she had stirred something deep inside of him. He shrugged it off. After all, it had been a long time since he had been in the company of a woman, a very beautiful woman.

He turned into the mobile home park and pulled in back of Billy's red truck. The home sat under a huge oak tree dripping with Spanish moss providing needed shade from the sizzling sun. Walking beside Billy's bed of petunias, struggling to survive, he stepped up to the screen door and let himself in.

The living room reverberated from the engines of race cars careening around a track. Billy had the television blaring with lap 82 of the day's NASCAR race. Billy and Lenny looked up at Razor as he passed the couch, then back to the TV screen.

"Help yourself to a beer and come join us," Billy said.

"Thanks, but I just dropped by to pick up my stuff. I rented a condo this morning, so I'll be leaving you two knuckleheads. How's the job going, Lenny? You keeping your nose clean?"

When Razor said he was moving out, Lenny jumped up and followed him to the bedroom.

"I'm doing okay. You leaving for good, Razor? I mean when will I see you? Will we be leaving Daytona Beach?"

"I'll see you again, but *we* won't be leaving Daytona Beach, at least not together. You're on your own. If you don't like your job, keep your eyes open for something else. Don't quit without having another job lined up."

"I'm not quitting. You know ... it's something, Razor, how people walk out of their houses around here, drive off, never locking their doors. Some of those big houses ... I could walk in the back door, lift a few pieces of jewelry and be long gone, blowing leaves off a driveway down the block before they came back."

"Lenny!"

"Ah, Razor, just kidding. I said I could. Not would." Lenny chuckled. "One of the guys on the lawn crew, him and me joke about it. He's real nice. Picks me up in the morning, and we stop for a beer on the way home most days."

"You watch yourself at work and pretty soon you'll be picking him up," Razor said gathering his toiletries off the bottom shelf of the bathroom closet.

"Razor, you remember how you showed me how to use the computer back at Folsom?"

"Sure I do. What about it?"

"Billy has a computer and I asked him if I could use it. This guy, my friend who picks me up, was talking about meeting girls. You know, one of those dating places on the internet."

"Go on."

"We thought we might give it a try. Him and me could double date." Lenny beamed at Razor as he divulged what he was up to.

"Just take it easy, Lenny. Girls can be trouble. Expensive trouble."

———

RAZOR MADE SEVERAL TRIPS to his second-floor condo transferring the suitcases Bull had packed for him. Hanging his sport coat in the closet along with his trousers, smoothing out the soft fabric, he then changed into a pair of chinos and a black golf shirt.

In no time at all he was sitting out in the balmy evening air on his balcony overlooking the ocean, martini in hand as several pelicans dove into the waves for their evening meal. A waft of air touched his cheek and his thoughts turned to Victoria. *She's one beautiful woman,* he thought. *Her husband's crazy not to pay attention to her. Some guy could come along and steal her away.*

Setting his drink on the glass table, he leaned down and opened his portfolio case next to his deck chair. Removing the pad, he turned to the sketch he had drawn of Victoria at the bookstore. Staring into her eyes, he felt the same pull he experienced earlier, something drawing him to her. He put the sketch back in his case, took another sip of the martini, and stared out at the waves crashing as they approached the shore.

He let his mind wander back to the bookstore. *I wonder what it would be like to live with a beautiful woman, a woman like Victoria, in a spot like this. The ocean lying out in front of us … meeting the horizon. Why do this job? Why not walk away? I have money. Because Pit Bull would hunt me down. I know too much about his so-called businesses. I have to take care of him before he turns against me. And, Razor, my friend, you know he will turn.*

Razor stood, put his hands on the railing, looked down at the white sand shining in the moonlight. His stomach slowly tightened in a knot. He swung away from the gentle lapping of the waves. The moment was lost. Thinking of Pit Bull, he was once again filled with hate and revenge at the price he paid to keep Bull out of prison. Eleven years. Too much.

He tried to sleep but sleep eluded him. He tossed and turned, the hours lasting forever. Finally, the sun breached the horizon. Razor showered, shaved, and dressed quickly. Looking in the yellow pages of the phone book he found an art supply store. They opened at nine o'clock.

He was at their entrance when a woman unlocked the plate-glass door. Following the woman's directions, he strode to the section displaying the items he needed. Filling the shopping cart, he checked out and left the strip mall. He made a quick stop at the Dunkin Donuts' drive-thru window, ordering a large coffee and two muffins. Placing the sack with his breakfast on the passenger seat, he drove out of the driveway and back to his condo.

Thoughts of Bull vanished. The stomach distress released. Adrenalin raced through Razor's body as he set up his easel and laid out his paints and brushes on the little table he had moved in front of the sliding glass doors to his balcony and the ocean beyond. Removing the sketchpad from his case, he gazed at the drawing, holding it out in front of him, sipping his coffee, taking a bite of muffin. Then he set to work creating a watercolor portrait of Victoria from the sketch he drew of her the day before ... the scarf softly framing her graceful neck. Her eyes, he had to capture her violet eyes gazing out at him.

Chapter 14

—

THE MORNING SUN WAS white hot with three days to go before the Fourth of July celebration. Polly walked through the bed of roses, deadheading the flowers that had turned brown. Her mind was elsewhere and she chided herself for pinching a beautiful, creamy-white Peace rose in its prime. "That's it, Regina. I have to call Liz. Tell her about my date this afternoon with a guitarist. Maybe she can check him out before I meet him." Regina sat on the lawn watching her mistress, dusting the grass with her tail.

Polly returned to the kitchen thankful for air conditioning and floated the Peace rose in a cocktail glass filled with an inch of cold water. Verifying Liz's telephone number anchored to the refrigerator with a little magnetic palm tree, she placed the call. The answering machine picked up wishing Polly a happy Fourth of July holiday.

"Hi, Liz, Polly Pringle here. I have a date this afternoon, 4:30, at the Manatee Oasis. I know, it's a bar, but I told the gentleman I only wanted a cup of coffee because I was invited out to dinner by a neighbor. How's that for an alibi? I'm learning. If you get a chance to look him up, his name is SunyBoy, one word with a capital S and B, Cashman. However, he shortened his last name to Cash. He plays the guitar and says his first name is really Sol but he liked SunyBoy for a stage name. He says he's sixty-nine, almost seventy. Sorry about the complicated name. Bye."

—

THERE WERE A COUPLE of cars and three motorcycles in the parking lot of the Manatee Oasis when Polly drove in. Once inside, she gave her eyes a chance to acclimate to the dim lighting, looking around for her date. A hostess, dressed in a white blouse with a name tag, over red shorts and a wide smile, hustled out from the back of the bar and asked Polly if she was staying for dinner?

"No, but I am meeting someone. A man. By any chance did SunyBoy leave his name with you, Dolly?"

"Oh, SunyBoy is a regular. A regular character," Dolly said laughing. "He told me he was expecting a lady. Follow me. He's sitting in his usual spot, up by the stage. We keep a mic hooked up so when he gets the urge to strum and sing he can sit up there and perform. Folks love him."

As Dolly approached a booth overlooking the small stage, a head popped up with a black patch over one eye. The head then disappeared.

"That's SunyBoy, honey," Dolly whispered. "I told you he was a character. Hey, SunyBoy, your lady friend is here."

SunyBoy stood, took one look at Polly and grinned from ear to ear. "Now, aren't you a pretty little lady. Dolly, bring us a couple of beers will ya?"

"Oh, coffee for me, please." Polly smiled at Dolly, who smiled at SunyBoy, who grinned at Polly.

"Make that one beer and one coffee, baby doll."

Dolly bustled off, her derriere swinging.

"Polly, can you sing?" SunyBoy asked sliding back onto the seat.

"Awhile back I sang in the church choir." Polly settled into the booth sitting opposite SunyBoy. Looking around she took note of the stage draped with red-white-and-blue bunting and glittery gold stars twirling from the ceiling.

"Well, that's a start. I thought we might sing *God Bless America* for the folks—after I have my beer. Gotta grease the pipes first," he said slapping his leg as he laughed. "Have you traveled much ... you know Nashville, Branson?"

"Nashville once. How about you?"

"Oh, I've been all over. Even Vegas."

Dolly brought their drinks and a bowl of pretzels to share. "You just wave me down, SunyBoy, if you and the lady want something else."

"I sure will, Dolly, and thanks for the pretzels."

"What happened to your eye," Polly asked. "That's quite a patch."

"Nothing really." SunyBoy lifted the patch, moving his eyes back and forth, and then covered his eye again. Leaning forward, he whispered, "I only wear it when I'm performing. Gives me a certain air don't you think?"

"Oh, yes. It adds to your costume—the boots and leather vest ... the billowy white sleeves along with the black patch makes you look like a pirate," Polly whispered back.

The bar began to fill up with laughter, along with a jukebox playing at full tilt adding to the festivities. Polly was pretty sure she wasn't going to be seeing SunyBoy again, but she found him entertaining and mused it was a bang up way to start the holiday. SunyBoy ordered another beer and persuaded Polly to drink one with him.

Dolly hustled back with their second round of drinks plus an order of potato skins topped with melted cheese. The party was in full swing when suddenly SunyBoy jumped up on the stage with his guitar and tapped the mic for attention.

"Nice to see you all here celebrating the birth of our country. I'm celebrating with a lovely lady. Her name is Polly. Polly, this is for you."

With that short introduction, he burst forth with a rousing rendition of The Saints Come Marching In. His foot tapped, fingers strummed, and the Manatee Oasis bar shook as everyone sang along with SunyBoy. At the end of the song everyone clapped and shouted for more, but SunyBoy said he had to get back to his little Polly. Dolly set two more bottles of beer on the table. "That was wonderful, SunyBoy," she gushed. "These are on the house."

"Why thank you, my little doll." Taking a swig, he turned to Polly. "I was thinking, Polly, we could have some fun traveling around together, you know in a trailer. You could dress in those cute little jeans with the jewels on your backside, a vest to go with, and well, hell, you could sell your house, buy us a trailer, and we would have us a merry old time."

"Oh, oh ... I don't think—"

"Polly. Polly Pringle, I bet you thought you could get away from me," Liz said as she strode up to SunyBoy's booth. Dressed all in black, including black trousers and shoes, she appeared to be a lawman. Without breaking her stride, Liz took Polly's arm and half lifted her up. Polly, immediately grasping that Liz had come to rescue her, stood up on her own.

"Liz, I suppose your being here means I'm going to jail for back payments of my taxes. I've already lost my house. This is awful. Bye, SunyBoy. Thanks for the drinks and good luck with your tour," Polly called out over her shoulder. "Let's go, Liz. I think the saints have marched in to cart me off."

———

MEETING BACK AT POLLY'S house, she replayed her date for Liz over a cup of tea. "Honestly, Liz, I'm sure everyone in the bar thought you were arresting me. I was never so happy to see anyone in my life as you marching up, practically throwing me over your shoulder, and hauling me away."

"The look on SunyBoy's face when you threw out the words that you were being arrested was priceless," Liz said, laughing with Polly.

"When I didn't hear from you this afternoon, I decided to go meet him, anyway. Whatever did you find out that made you come after me?"

"I checked with my friend, Manny Salinas. He's a captain at the Daytona Beach Police Department. He found your SunyBoy. He has a rap sheet a mile long, and I don't mean rap like in songs. Mainly for embezzling money from women."

"Well, I guess I'll send SunyBoy a *Dear John* message tonight. Although I doubt he wants to hear from me ... a tax evader. More tea?"

Chapter 15

—

Yahoo, July 2nd, From: Victoria Brookfield

"Hi, Richard, I'm going to Barnes and Noble this morning about eleven. Want to meet for coffee? Your friend, Victoria."

Gmail, July 2nd, From: Richard Stiles

"I'll be there. Richard"

Victoria was browsing in the art section of the bookstore, looking for a book on the techniques of painting with watercolors and oils, when she felt a soft touch on her arm. A shot of electricity ran to her heart as she touched the man's fingers. She quickly pulled her hand away and looked up at Richard. This was the third time they had met in the last eight days—twice in a café for lunch and then coffee, and now in the bookstore where he had sketched her portrait although he still hadn't shown it to her. Each time she didn't want to leave him and anxiously looked forward to seeing him again.

He was standing much too close. She took a half step back. "How are you? You're just in time to help me decide which book to buy."

"I'm fine, but is the traffic always this bad?"

"The holiday," she said smiling. "It's always a little crazy this time of morning but around a holiday with fireworks and a NASCAR race, watch out. So, which one should I buy?" She asked showing him three books.

Taking the books from her hands he perused the table of contents of each. As he thumbed through, he asked, "And the reason you picked these particular books is?"

"I have a collection by various artists, mostly the impressionist period—Monet, Renoir, and others. Watching you sketch the first time we met, started me thinking that I should study the methods and techniques of various artists—to understand more about their paintings."

Richard handed the books back to her, ran his fingers over the bindings of the books on the shelves in front of them, pulled one out, pushed it back, then selected another. "Here, I'll buy this one for you, and I think you'll find what you're looking for in the three you have in your hands."

"Thanks." She looked at him, hesitated, not sure if she wanted to say what she was thinking.

"What?" he asked grinning. "Something's going on in that head of yours."

"Well ... you're new to the area, and people are gearing up for the 4th holiday. Have you been to the arcades along the beach, off Main Street?"

"No. Want to show me? Can we get a Coney Island red hot?"

"And, an ice cream cone. I'll meet you there."

"Can't we go together?"

"I think it's best if we drive in separate cars."

———

RICHARD FOLLOWED HER gray sedan and parked a few cars away from hers. Locking up he joined her on the sidewalk. The beach was packed with umbrellas, beach chairs, kids building sandcastles, and surfers paddling frantically to catch the next big wave. A hammer concession sent the riders screaming into the air, plunging down, then up again.

The arcades, food stalls, and souvenir stands were doing a brisk business, music blaring from high-powered speakers.

"Wow, I haven't seen a Fourth of July celebration for a long time. I had no idea this was here—all these people. Some are inviting serious sunburns."

"You should see it on the Fourth. They will be lying bumper to bumper."

"Is that supposed to be a joke?" he asked grinning.

"Let's get something to eat. Hot dogs are—"

"What?" his voiced raised.

"I said hot dogs are in the next shop," she yelled over a gyrating jukebox.

Richard moved to take her hand but she quickly tucked her arms across her chest. He bought four hotdogs and then they muscled their way to the ketchup, mustard, and relish counter.

"Let's get out of here," he yelled. "How about walking in the surf while we eat?"

She nodded, took a bite of her hot dog, and closed her eyes. "Heavenly," she said mouthing the word.

Guiding her out of the crowd, they meandered through the sunbathers to the water. Victoria slipped off her white sandals sticking them in a side pocket of her shoulder bag. Richard tied his shoelaces together and tossed them over his shoulder. The water lapping over the hot sand felt warm on their feet. Neither talked. Victoria finished her hot dog, declining with a nod a second. *It's a beautiful day to be on the beach*, she thought.

"That sun is blistering," Richard said rinsing mustard off his fingers in the water. "I don't suppose I could interest you in a cold drink at my condo?"

"Your condo? In Orlando? I think—"

"No, no. I didn't like the hotel and with all the snowbirds going north, I was able to get a short-term rental. It's not far from here … and it's on the water."

"Well, I am about to burn. Just one though."

"You follow me this time, but in case we get separated, it's a three-story, pink building—The Ocean View Tower. Not too original," he said with a grin.

———

FUMBLING WITH HIS keys, Richard opened the door, nodding for her to go in. "It came furnished—not too bad, huh? The sun is now behind us so we can have our drinks on the balcony. I think there'll be a breeze. What would you like—beer, wine, rum and coke?"

"Rum and coke sounds great—light on the rum."

Victoria noticed the easel standing beside the sliding glass door to the balcony. A blank canvas stretched on a wooden frame leaned against it. She slid the door open and stepped out onto the narrow balcony taking in the expansive view of the ocean—a cargo ship was riding on the horizon.

"Here you are—one coke with rum on the light side," he said handing her a highball glass. He tipped his glass of beer to hers. "I told you—a nice cool breeze. I hope we see some pelicans. It's just about the time of day they fly by and dive into the water. Hey, here comes one—make that three." He leaned into her arm, pointing to their right.

"I've seen them from a restaurant but never up close like this. They're so big. Beautiful." She turned to look at him but he was so close she could feel his breath on her cheek. "I have to go. This wasn't a good idea."

She stood, inched passed him and walked inside. Setting her drink on the counter, she picked up her purse and turned to face him. "Thanks, but—"

Richard took a step closer to her, raised her chin and softly kissed her lips. Lifting his head he watched her open her eyes. They both felt the heat rising in their bodies.

Victoria turned, opened the front door, closing it gently behind her as she left.

Chapter 16

—

THE HOLIDAY WAS OVER and Daytona Beach residents hid out in their homes with air conditioning on high as temperatures pushed up over ninety-five degrees with a heat index above a hundred.

Polly called an emergency quilting session so the group could knuckle down and sew the finishing stitches on the quilt. The regional director for Quilts of Valor had called again, pleading with Polly to send the quilt by the end of the week.

Adding lemon wedges and a dash of sugar to the pitcher of ice tea, Polly went to answer the doorbell. Giving each quilter a hug, they entered the cool house. Polly waved at Billy who was distributing more mulch on the flower beds trying to save every last bit of moisture for the plants. A helper, opening the bags, looked up at Polly with a big grin spreading across his face.

Back in the dining room, the girls helped themselves to iced tea, each putting her glass on a table behind her to prevent an accident. They all gave Kelly a wide birth.

The group was unusually quiet—each quilter intent on finishing her section. Polly sat down and threaded her needle.

"I had another date a few days ago," she said, pulling bright lemon yellow thread through the fabric.

"Why didn't you tell me?" Mildred chastised. She adjusted her thimble and took another stitch.

"What was he like, Mrs. P?" Kelly kept her head down and continued to sew.

"He was interesting. A singer. SunyBoy. He played the guitar and serenaded me."

"Sounds romantic," Kelly said. "Are you going to see him again?"

"Mercy, no. He wanted me to sell my house, buy a trailer, and go on tour with him."

"You'd better be careful, Polly Pringle. He could have mugged you," Mildred said, looking at her with tight lips, her eyebrows drawn together.

"Not likely. I have a saint watching over me."

"Balderdash," Mildred hissed. "A saint!"

Susan kept sewing, paused a moment when Polly said the date wanted her to sell her house, and then continued stitching.

"No one seems to be in a talkative mood today," Polly quipped. "How's your wrist, Kelly?"

"Getting better." Kelly made a final stitch, snipping the thread next to the knot. Carol's ringtone quacked and Kelly fished her phone out of her shorts pocket. She picked up her glass of tea and walked into the kitchen for a private conversation. A sound of crashing wood on the tile floor emanated from the kitchen. Polly jumped up." Oh dear, I didn't tuck the stool under the counter. Kelly must have walked right into it," she said hustling out of the room.

Kelly was still talking on the phone, rubbing her knee, when Polly came to her aid picking up the stool.

"You okay?" Polly asked.

Kelly nodded, yes. "I'll be back in a jiff."

Polly shook her head and returned to the dining room. The group, all dressed in jeans and white Ts, with the exception of Mildred in another flowered house dress and a blue apron, helped Polly smooth out the quilt on the table, then stood back admiring their handiwork.

"It's beautiful isn't it?" Polly said, a slight catch in her throat. "I'll send it off tomorrow. The director said she'd send us a picture of the soldier when she presents it to him. She didn't say anything about his wounds, but he'll know we care about him."

"It's the least we can do," Mildred said wiping away a tear. "Will we sew another one?" she asked.

"If you want to. Maybe we could find a couple more quilters—expand our group," Polly suggested.

Kelly's phone quacked again and the melancholy moment evaporated. Glaring at Kelly, Susan excused herself and left the house. Mildred carried the empty iced-tea pitcher to the kitchen and scooted out the back door, bypassing Billy.

———

"LENNY, STOP GAWKING and hand me another bag of that mulch," Billy yelled, his hands reaching out.

"Okay, okay. Don't get your drawers in a knot," Lenny yelled back. In a softer voice, he added, "That last woman, the one who drove off in that red convertible, she's a real looker ain't she, Billy?"

"Forget it. She's a stuck-up socialite. Susan Armstrong. She lives in a mansion on the ocean," Billy said watching the convertible turn the corner out of sight.

———

POLLY FOLDED THE QUILT and carefully maneuvered it into the pillowcase tube she had sewn together before they started the project. Taking the tube, which looked like a sleeping-bag carrier, to her guest bedroom, she placed it in a cardboard box and taped it shut.

Noting her computer was still on she decided to check if there were any new messages in her account at SeniorFriendFinder.

A message from a new gentleman had arrived, and another one from Sam in response to hers of a few days ago. She had told Sam about her date with the guitarist, and he in turn told her of his experience with a lady whose picture looked quite nice. However, she turned out to be fifteen years older than the picture, had gained thirty pounds, and was looking for a man she could move in with. Sam wrote he liked the way Polly cut off the question of future dates quickly if things didn't work out. He said he sent her a "Dear Joan" message the next morning.

Polly didn't like the looks of the man who sent the first message so she deleted it without replying.

"So easy. No sticky situation. Just delete him," she said to Regina who had curled up on her lap. Polly clicked on the small television on the bedside table to check the latest weather update.

"This is Channel 13 news at noon.

It's been a week since the 4th of July heat wave. If you haven't put together your hurricane kits now is the time to get those supplies. Go to our website for a list of items you should have on hand as well as family communication and evacuation plans.

The U.S. National Hurricane Center issued a statement this morning that a tropical depression, with sustained winds of thirty-three miles per hour, had formed over the Bahamas a few days ago. Updating that report, a tropical storm watch is issued for portions of the Florida Keys and the Gulf Coast. At present, the sustained winds have increased from a range of thirty-nine to fifty-two miles per hour. Peak gusts are stronger.

Oil and gas prices jumped yesterday with word that energy production on the Gulf Coast could be disrupted.

Again we suggest you visit our website for a list of supplies to have on hand in case your power is interrupted.

We received the following question from George on FaceBook: When does a storm receive a name?

Well, George, once a tropical storm develops, it earns a name from a list selected by the World Meteorological Organization. If a really destructive hurricane hits, such as Andrew or Katrina, the name is never used again.

This is the season when it pays to be alert to potential storm systems coming our way. Stay tuned for further updates on the path of this storm.

We now take you to the traffic report."

Chapter 17

—

SITTING AT HER COMPUTER, Regina on her lap, Polly tapped the send button accepting a date with Tom Hunt. She had corresponded with him several times over the last few days. He seemed very nice and had signed off his last message with his full name. She smiled, picked up the yellow notepad on her desk and finished the list of the day's chores. Looking up she saw a message from Sam had just been deposited in her inbox. He chatted about a squirrel he had befriended. The little fellow was now eating a few bits of squirrel food he purchased, so he named him Nugget. He wished her a happy day.

How nice, she thought, smiling as she stroked Regina's fur.

She glanced at the other chores on her list and then placed a call to Liz. She gave her Tom Hunt's name, that he lived in Daytona Beach, was a retired financial analyst but still helped a few clients. He had also given her his cell number. Liz said she would do a quick check and get back to her by one o'clock. Tom had suggested they meet for an after-lunch drink at 2:00. "Let's skip the coffee thing," he wrote.

Liz called back thirty minutes later and reported that a Tom Hunt did live in Daytona Beach, and she found that he had been in finance working for an investment firm in Orlando. However, there seemed to be an age discrepancy—he was not seventy-two, as he had led Polly to believe, but sixty-two.

"That's about it, Polly. I'd be wary—maybe set up an excuse that you have to leave by three o'clock. If he's legit, you can always meet him again if you want to. I did check with Rocket and he didn't know the name, but then there are a lot of financial consultants so he wasn't surprised that the name Tom Hunt didn't ring a bell."

"Thanks, Liz. He seemed so sad in his emails—lost his wife six months ago and is looking for someone to talk to."

"Be careful. That's all I'm saying. Remember, don't give him any personal information including your last name. Where are you meeting?"

"At Stonewood, on Dunlawton Avenue."

———

POLLY STEPPED INTO THE restaurant at exactly two o'clock. The hostess asked if she would like a table in the dining room.

"No," Polly said peering around the corner into the bar. "I'm meeting a gentleman for a drink. I know what he looks like but it's the first time we're meeting in person," Polly said, looking at the hostess. Apprehension showed on Polly's face but the hostess smiled, "I think the gentleman came in about ten minutes ago. Over there. In the booth. Is that the guy?"

"Oh, yes," Polly said. She wondered if the apprehension over meeting a blind date would ever abate. Following the hostess, she sucked in a lungful of air, straightened her posture, and pasted a smile on her face.

"Sir," the hostess said, "I believe I have the lady you were looking for."

"Good. Hello, Polly, your picture doesn't do you justice," Tom said, standing to greet her. "Please, have a seat."

Polly released the breath she was holding and, with a genuine smile, slipped into the booth opposite Tom Hunt.

"Can I get you two a bite to eat? Something to drink?" The hostess was almost giddy seeing the pair in front of her. "I think it's so nice you two reaching out … at your age and all," she said looking more at Polly than Tom.

"Polly, what would you like to drink?" Tom asked.

"I think a glass of Chardonnay, please. I have a group meeting later and I don't want to be tipsy."

"Oh, I'm sorry. Not about the wine but about the meeting. I'd hoped we might have an early dinner." Tom looked from Polly to the hostess. "I'll have a martini and … how about an order of your stuffed mushrooms. Is that okay with you?" he asked, looking at Polly.

"Yes, that would be nice."

The hostess left to get their order and Tom launched into a story about his car problems.

He seems pleasant. Looks like his picture, but I think Liz is right, he's closer to sixty-two than seventy-two. Still, he's very attentive. Polly found herself laughing and after a couple of sips of wine, she began to relax. He spoke a little about his wife and asked Polly about her husband, how long she'd been in Florida, and commented on how hard it was to live alone after being married for so many years.

Polly was enjoying their conversation and later talking to Liz she couldn't say exactly when she began to notice little things about him. Things that seemed slightly off. He presented himself as a professional, yet he definitely could have used a haircut. It wasn't that it was long, but more like he had trimmed it himself. Then there were the two missing gold buttons on his blazer. The conversation seemed to falter a little and Polly took the opportunity to look at her watch.

"Tom, I've had a very nice time but I do have to be going." She reached into her pocket for the ten-dollar bill she had put there to pay her portion of the tab, or close enough. No dime in the shoe like her mother had always insisted she carry. Inflation hits everything, she had giggled when Liz suggested she keep some money where she could get at it easily rather than in her wallet.

Tom didn't say anything about her contribution, only added enough to cover the bill—no tip. Polly, now more than slightly alarmed, got up to say goodbye.

"I'll walk you to your car, Polly. I hope we can do this again soon," he said.

Only a few cars remained in the parking lot. Working men and women returning to their jobs after a quick lunch out, Polly surmised. She opened her car door and turned to again thank Tom for meeting with her but he stepped in, put his hands gently on her shoulders and drew her in for a kiss.

"Tom, this is too—"

He grasped her in an ardent embrace. The vision of Detective Miles demonstrating how to handle a frontal attack flashed through her mind. Seeing the detective, she instinctively did what he told his students to do. Polly whipped her body back then forward into a headbutt. At the same time, with all her strength she jammed her knee into his crotch. Tom, startled, doubled over, crying out in pain. Polly jumped into her car slamming the door which automatically snapped the locks tight.

With shaky fingers, she quickly started the car, backed out of the parking space, and sped away.

———

TURNING INTO HER DRIVEWAY, Polly tapped the garage door opener, drove in and tapped the button again. The door slid down its tracks safely enclosing her within cement-block walls. She sat motionless, going over in her mind what happened. "Polly," she whispered, "what are you doing? Meeting a man online, thinking … thinking he was going to be prince charming. This is ridiculous. Stop it. Stop it now!"

She climbed out of the car and limped into the house. Her head hurt and her knee felt a little out of whack, but other than that she had survived Tom's advance unscathed. Her phone rang as she set her purse down on the counter.

"Hello."

"Polly, it's Liz. Are you all right? You sound funny. How did—"

"It was a disaster. Meeting a man this way … well, it's too fast, not real. You fall into an intimate conversation after you say, 'how do you do, I'm doing fine,' and—"

"Polly, what happened?"

"He put the make on me in the parking lot. But, I retaliated with one of Detective Miles' self-defense tactics. I think Mr. Tom Hunt will think twice before he tries to move in so fast with another woman."

Chapter 18

—

VICTORIA'S WORLD WAS IN a state of confusion. Richard filled her every thought. Harri was busy with his design work, so what harm could there be if she had a casual friend … to talk to … to laugh with … someone who thought she was charming, witty, pretty. The problem was that casual had turned hot. She wasn't sure how it happened—coffee one morning, then lunch a day later, then mid-afternoon drinks in a little bar on the beach-side of Port Orange. His hand across the table, holding her hand, then his kiss the day she left his condo sending shock waves through her body.

She paced from room to room—kitchen, bedroom, study. The late afternoon sun painted shadows on the walls. *I have to stop this. No more rendezvous.* "Oh, Richard, what have we done?" she whispered. But she knew she couldn't, wouldn't stop meeting him. She had to see him again. He touched off a spark that now flamed inside her. She poured herself a stiff drink of vodka over ice hoping it would settle her nerves. *Maybe he'll see the futility of our friendship. Tell me he doesn't want to see me anymore. He knows I'm married. I've made it clear that I'm not free to act on my feelings for him.*

Sipping her drink, she turned on the computer and logged into her FaceBook account. A message was waiting for her. A message from Richard. She knew there would be. He was now sending her several a day. Her hand shaking, she clicked to open it.

"Victoria, meet me tomorrow afternoon. You sound
frustrated. Let me hold your hand. Help you to visualize a

brighter horizon. I must see you. My place. Two o'clock.
Yours, Richard"

Yours. Yes.
If he wanted her tomorrow, she would be his.

———

THE MOMENT HE HIT the send button Richard knew he'd made a mistake.

"What in God's name was I thinking," he yelled, stomping through the living room into the kitchen, down the hall to the bedroom, and back again.

"You've made stupid moves before, Razor. But inviting Victoria here again? The one place she should never have known about? Where I live? It was a mistake. You weren't thinking. And now you've made another blunder."

Razor yanked open the slider to his balcony. Gripping the railing with both hands, he leaned forward, closed his eyes and saw Victoria.

"Shit. Shit. Shit. I have to pull this job now before I ruin everything. You think you're falling for this woman? Well, think again, buster. She's your ticket to retirement. The good life. Going straight—no more looking over your shoulder, no more jobs, no more Bull. Yea, keep his pudgy face in your mind. Forget Victoria."

Razor poured a stiff drink. Swirling the scotch around the ice, he headed to the bathroom to shower. He had to stay focused. His future depended on it, maybe even his life.

———

HEARING A LIGHT RAP, Richard opened the door and Victoria fell into his arms. Shoving the door shut with his foot, he held her against him smothering her with urgent kisses, each one hotter than the last. His resolve blurred and then was swept away with renewed passion.

"Victoria, will you let me make love to you?" he whispered in her ear even as he carried her to the bedroom.

Victoria didn't reply—caught up in her own desires, guilt, wants, needs. Her eyes told him she wanted him as much as he wanted her. She slowly pulled her silky, sky-blue dress up over her head and let it drop to the floor.

Watching her, seeing her beautiful body covered with only a white satin teddy, he again took her in his arms and kissed her gently. He lifted her and slowly, slowly, laid her down on the bed. Ripping his clothes off, never taking his eyes from her, he laid next to her, pulling her to him.

"You must leave your husband." His voice raspy, strangled in his throat.

"I can't," she said moaning with desire as his hand roamed over her curves.

"Victoria, I can give you a better life. I have money. I'm retiring. We'll go far away."

Her skin was creamy ... it had been so long ... so long ... he felt himself dip deep into her womanhood savoring her ardent response.

On and on they loved, touched, kissed until she screamed his name and he hers. Even then not stopping, sweat trickling from every pore until finally ... finally ... finally they parted, laid back exhausted ... minds blank. Years of pent-up emotion and desire released from their bodies.

"Victoria, my dear Victoria. Forgive me for the brusqueness of my message yesterday but I had to hold you, to see your beautiful face, touch your silky black hair, look into your eyes and see that you are feeling the same. I haven't been with a woman for many years, had no desire to be. Then you entered my life."

———

ENTERED HIS LIFE? Victoria slowly rolled away from Richard's embrace. Trembling, she picked up her clothes, went into the bathroom and shut the door. Clutching the sink, she looked at her reflection in the mirror. She had crossed the line.

"Can I step back?" she asked the woman in the mirror. The woman looked different. She wasn't the person who left her home a few hours earlier.

"My home? You have no home now. You violated Harri's trust. I'll ask him to forgive me. But then I'd have to tell him … tell him why I want to be forgiven."

Victoria turned the shower on as hot as she could stand it, hoping it would wash away the guilt. She planted the palms of her hands against the tile wall as the tears began to flow, then choking sobs. Sliding down the tile wall she sat on the floor of the shower, water beating her hair and skin.

"I don't love you, Harri. I don't love you," she cried out. "I feel alive for the first time in my life … with a stranger."

Sobs continued to rack her body. Then a little less. And then she began to regain control—the sobs, then the tears stopped. She stood up and turned off the faucet. Toweling off … she looked at the woman in the mirror and didn't recognize her. The woman's eyes were red and swollen, her hair hanging damp in soft waves, her being filled with forbidden desire.

Victoria turned away, dressed quickly, and left the bathroom. The bed was made and Richard was gone. She heard the gurgling of the coffee maker and followed the aroma.

Richard was standing at the sink. Hearing her footsteps, he turned and faced her, his face devoid of emotion. Cold. He opened his mouth to speak but Victoria hastily put her finger to his lips stopping him.

"What just happened was a dream," she said. "We both wanted something and what we got must remain a secret—only you and I will ever know how much it meant, each in a different way. But I will never come here again. I'd like to think we might meet for coffee sometime, but not for a while."

Victoria looked into his eyes. The cold look a moment ago was gone. She saw he was as tortured as she. Picking up her purse, she turned and walked out the door closing it softly behind her as before.

———

RICHARD WATCHED HER go. Rooted to the floor. His head dropped. His arms, that had held her a short time ago, hung limp at his side.

Taking a deep breath, he snatched his sketchpad from its case, strode to the bedroom and climbed on the bed. Leaning against the headboard, he attacked the pad—long, quick strokes. His eyes bore into the paper seeing only his subject. Taking form in front of him was Victoria, her head on the pillow looking back at him. The sheet was tight against her body revealing every curve. More strokes. Erasing a line. Stroking again. Finally, his hand fell to his side.

Satisfied he had captured her. The moment. He leaned his head back closing his eyes. His breathing returned to normal.

"I'll move out of here tomorrow."

With the scent of Victoria's perfume lingering in the air, he rolled slowly out of bed. Picking up the sketchpad he pressed it to his chest. He walked to the balcony but turned away. The beauty of the ocean below was too much for his battered senses. Reaching for the remote, he turned on the television hoping for a distraction.

"This is Channel 13 News at 4:01.

Terry, what do you have for us on tropical storm Bonnie?"

"Yesterday's tropical storm watch has been extended. The weather trackers report Bonnie is likely to be upgraded to a Category 1 hurricane and is on a slow moving, erratic course through the Gulf of Mexico. It's too early to say where she might make landfall but projections show anywhere from Louisiana, east to the Florida panhandle in two to four days depending on her speed.

We'll be giving updates every two hours and more often as Bonnie moves closer."

"Thanks, Terry. And now for a report on Florida's budget deliberations."

Turning off the TV, Razor squared his shoulders, straightened his spine, and began packing his suitcase. It was time to start executing his plan.

Chapter 19

KELLY TURNED INTO THE medical facility and parked her silver-gray PT Cruiser, her parent's present to her for achieving straight A's her junior year of high school. In Florida, as a sixteen-year-old, she was restricted from driving after dark for the first three months after obtaining her license and after 10:00 p.m. for twelve months. She posted a quick note on her FaceBook wall before getting out of the car:

> "About to have an interview for a part-time job after school this fall. Wish me luck. Then Mom and I are going shopping at Macy's and out to dinner."

She signed out and went into the medical building.

Sitting in the small, personnel waiting room for her appointment, Kelly took a quick look at her phone to see if anyone had commented on her FaceBook post. There was one comment. Carol wished her good luck.

Kelly didn't notice the shadow behind the filmy curtain that faced the reception desk. Even if she had, it wouldn't have occurred to her that she was being watched. The secretary stood and smiled. "Kelly, Mrs. Jordan will see you now," she said opening the office door for Kelly to enter.

"Thanks," Kelly replied returning the smile. She popped her cell into her jacket pocket, picked up her leather folder, straightened her emerald green skirt, and walked in for her interview.

Diane Jordan, the head of the hospital's Human Resource staff, welcomed her with a handshake and a nod to take a seat in the chair facing her desk. Kelly handed her an additional copy of her resume. She had dropped one off the week before at the time she made the appointment, but her father said she should be prepared with an additional copy. More professional.

"In your resume, you state that you plan to enter pre-med when you graduate next May," Diane said, looking up from the resume and over her glasses at Kelly.

"Yes, and that's one reason I applied here. My counselor told me you had a student-work program. I—" Kelly was interrupted with a sound of a quack. She snatched the cell out of her suit pocket and turned on the silencer. "Sorry. I forgot to turn my phone off."

Mrs. Jordan shot Kelly a piercing glance. "I looked earlier on FaceBook to see if you had an account. Something I do regularly to get a personal perspective of an applicant. You're quite active," she said with a thin smile.

"Yes, I guess so. My folks gave me a cell phone, a smartphone with lots of apps, for my birthday … for emergencies. It's still new to me, but a few of my friends also have smartphones and FaceBook is a fun way to keep in touch. Homework assignments, you know." Kelly shifted in her chair fidgeting with the strap on her purse. *Darn, Mom warned me to shut my phone off. Mrs. Jordan's looking at me kinda funny. I didn't think she'd check out my FaceBook posts. What did I—"*

Mrs. Jordan cut into Kelly's thoughts. "You understand, as a part-time employee, you will be assigned to various floors— wherever you're needed that day. But, because you're considering the medical field, do you have a preference?"

"Whatever you need is fine. Just working in the hospital will be incredibly helpful if I'm accepted into medical school. You asked if I had a preference. Any area where I could work with children, or the maternity ward with mothers and their babies, would be wonderful."

Mrs. Jordan asked her a couple of other questions about her availability and, before Kelly knew it, she was escorted out the door.

"Thanks for coming to see me, Kelly. I have several applicants and only two slots. I'll be making a decision by the end of next week."

Mrs. Jordan briskly returned to her office, closing the door behind her, leaving Kelly standing in front of the secretary's desk. Kelly looked at the young woman, straightened up and said goodbye.

Shaken, she walked down the hall to the elevator. "I blew it," she mumbled. "Mrs. Jordan didn't even give me a chance to thank her." Kelly felt her phone vibrate. It was Carol. She stuffed it back into her pocket. "For sure I'm not going to post anything about my interview. Mrs. Jordan is probably checking right now."

Leaving the building through the automatic sliding glass doors, Kelly saw an elderly woman pushing a man in a wheelchair. The man said something and the woman leaned over his shoulder to answer. As she talked the front wheel slid off the walkway into the grass tilting the chair at a precarious angle. Kelly hustled up to the couple dropping her purse on the grass by the chair.

"Here, let me help you," she said, grasping the arm of the wheelchair with both hands, lifting it back onto the walkway.

"Oh, thank goodness you came along, dear," the woman said.

"Yes, young lady, thank you. That's some set of muscles you have there," the man said chuckling.

Kelly smiled at the couple. "Can I help you with the door?"

"No. My driver can handle it. Can't you, sweetheart."

"Yes, as long as I keep your wheels straight. Thanks again, dear."

Kelly picked up her purse and watched them enter the building. Feeling better after helping the couple, she called her mother to let her know the interview was over and she would meet her at the mall in front of Macy's. Tossing her purse in the car, she slid in catching her image in the rearview mirror.

"She's never going to hire me. I didn't impress her, I could feel it."

Kelly turned the key in the ignition. I'll send her a thank you note, she thought. A personal note. Handwritten. Not an email.

Her spirits brightened as she began thinking about clothes shopping with her mom. They always had a good time with each other at the mall. Kelly pushed the image of Mrs. Jordan looking at her FaceBook postings out of her mind.

Chapter 20

—

THE MALL WAS ALWAYS busy in the late afternoon. Now, after four o'clock, mothers scurried with babies in strollers, children in tow, running errands before going home to fix dinner. Men and women dashed around after work before starting their evening activities.

Kelly pushed through the glass doors quickly blending in with the crowd. She veered off with several other shoppers heading to Macy's. Hearing her mother's call, she glanced around and spotted her mom sitting at a bistro table in the middle of a wide expanse of trees leading to the department store. Dodging a stroller, a woman with bundles under each arm, and an older couple meandering along window shopping, Kelly stepped quickly to her mother, gave her a hug, and flopped down in the black, wrought-iron chair.

"I thought we might have a glass of iced-coffee before we hit the store," Vicky said picking up her purse. "I'll go, but I want to hear how your interview went. Then we shop."

"Okay, Mom. Make mine cinnamon-ginger, please. I'll hold our table," Kelly said at the same time Carol's ringtone quacked. Vicky left, making her way to the deli's coffee counter. Kelly flipped open her phone and immediately became engrossed in an animated conversation.

"Victoria. Victoria, over here," Richard called backing around the edge of the coffee shop out of sight.

Victoria quickly walked around the corner to him. With a discreet kiss on her cheek, Richard picked up her hand and gently pulled her along with him toward one of the mall's exits.

"Richard, no, I'm meeting Kelly," she said. "Where are we going?"

"I had an idea ... I have to share it with you."

"Now?" she asked trying to keep pace with his long strides. "Are you psychic? How did you find me?" She was smiling, wondering where this game of his was leading. They had exchanged a few messages since the afternoon in his condo but they hadn't seen each other.

"I'm parked next to the curb. Just give me minute to explain."

Passing through the automatic, sliding-glass door, Victoria saw his car a few feet away. He opened the back door, nodded for her to get inside and he slid in beside her closing the door.

"Victoria—"

"Richard, I have to go back. Kelly's waiting for me."

"I know. Just hear me out ... Victoria ... I love you." He clasped her hands trying to convey his feelings, but he could see his timing was wrong. She wasn't listening to him.

"Oh, Richard ... not now. You know I—"

"Please, come away with me. You can let Kelly know where you are ... later ... I promise. I—"

"I can't. I have to go. How about coffee at the bookstore? Tomorrow."

"I'm sorry, but that will be too late." Richard closed his eyes a second, hesitated, then reached into his jacket pocket. Feeling around, he withdrew a damp rag from a plastic bag, quickly covered her nose. Holding the cloth in place, he put his other hand firmly behind her head. She gasped, a startled look spreading across her face, and then fell forward unconscious into his arms. He secured a gag over her mouth, and loosely tied her wrists together, and then her ankles.

Sliding out the car door, he reached in gently laying her head down on the backseat. He shut the door and jumped into the driver's side. Starting the engine he drove slowly out of the mall parking lot, merging into the heavy afternoon traffic.

———

KELLY ANSWERED CAROL'S barrage of questions as her friend quizzed her about the interview insisting on a word-for-word description of what happened. Kelly gave her the blow-by-blow and chastised Carol, with a giggle, for calling when she was in Mrs. Jordan's office.

"She practically told me I'd be emptying bedpans and then turned around and asked what floor, as if I had a choice, I would pick to work on."

"What did you tell her?" Carol asked.

"The same you and I talked about," Kelly replied. "With children. I did add the maternity ward, especially with the babies in the nursery. But, get this."

"What?"

"Something you'd better keep in mind, my friend. Mrs. Jordan had looked at my FaceBook postings."

"She said that?"

"Yes. I was mortified."

"How did she see what you posted?"

"What do you mean how?"

"Your account settings, silly," Carol said. "I set mine to private— only family and friends."

"I must have skipped that. I'll check. Anyway, Mrs. Jordan said I should hear about the job by next week."

Carol broke in about her new boyfriend, Brad. He had asked her out to the movies on Saturday night. He was tall, had red hair, and gorgeous.

"I wish I had a boyfriend," Kelly said. "But with my heavy class load coming up I guess it's just as well that I'm not involved. I'd better go, Carol. Mom should be here with our coffees. I'll text you if we find any spectacular outfits. I'm looking for a pair of white capris and a red tank top … and maybe a pair of red sandals to go with. Bye."

Kelly closed her phone and looked over at the coffee shop for her mother. She didn't see her so she settled back in her chair watching the shoppers rush here and there—her thoughts returning to the interview with Mrs. Jordan. Fifteen minutes went by and Kelly started to feel uneasy. She pulled her phone out of her pocket and punched the number she stored for her mom. She didn't answer. Kelly straightened up in her chair … then stood … looking around in all directions. Her pulse quickened. Her mother was nowhere in sight. She tried her cell again. No answer. She hit her dad's number.

"Hi, sweetie. How did the interview go?" Harri asked.

"It went okay. Dad, did mom call you?"

"No. Why?"

"I met her in front of Macy's. She went to get us a couple of iced-coffees and I haven't seen her since."

"Maybe she went into the store. Did you look?"

"No, but she didn't say she was going in."

"Had the two of you talked about what you were shopping for?"

"Yes. I wanted to look for a new pair of capris."

"Well, go to that department and have a look around. If you don't see her call me back."

"Okay. I'll do that. And I'll check with Polly. Maybe mom called her." Kelly ended the call with her dad and called Polly.

"Polly, it's Kelly—"

"Hello, dear. What a hot day."

"Yes, it is hot. By any chance did my mom call you in the last—" Kelly looked at her watch and was shocked at the time. It was almost 5:30. "Did she call you in the last hour? I can't find her."

"No, she hasn't called me. Where are you?"

"I'm at the mall—in front of Macy's. Dad said she didn't call him either. He suggested I take a look around the store and if I don't find her to call him back."

"That sounds like a good idea. Call me when you find her will you, Kelly?"

"Sure."

Kelly stuffed her phone in her pocket and ran into Macy's, up the escalator to the second floor, and into the young women's department. She darted in and out of the racks of blouses, dresses, pants of various lengths calling for her mother, hoping to find her around the next bend. Her heart racing, Kelly struggled to get her phone out of her jacket pocket dropping it on the carpet. She quickly bent down, picked it up and called her dad.

"Hello," a woman said. A stranger.

"I'm sorry, I have the wrong number." Kelly cut the call and tried her dad's code again.

"Where did you find her, honey?"

"I didn't find her." Kelly wiped away a tear escaping her eye. "I can't find her. She's disappeared. Dad, where is she?"

"I'm sure she's around there. Where are you now?" he asked.

"I'm in the store. Daddy, she's gone."

"Kelly, she's probably looking for you and the two of you are missing each other. I'll meet you in front of Macy's, south entrance. Stay there."

"Hurry, Dad."

Chapter 21

—

CLAMPING HIS FOOT DOWN on the gas pedal, Razor left the city limits of Daytona Beach. He exited I-95 North to Route 40 West. Less than an hour later he turned off onto a rural road, and again onto a dirt pathway. Flipping on the car radio he listened for any news that Victoria had been reported missing. The newscaster only commented on an impending storm that had been upgraded to a hurricane but was unlikely to pose any danger to central Florida. However, a glancing blow to the panhandle was likely.

He flicked the radio off, looked in his rearview mirror to be sure that Victoria was still out from the chloroform. "You're so paranoid, you dumb ass," he said chastising himself. "It's only a little more than an hour since you left the mall."

Hitting a rut he slowed the car, watching for the break in the trees leading to the trailer he'd rented. He would have to secure her inside, and then ditch the vehicle in case the surveillance cameras at the mall picked up his license plate. That depended on whether or not he was seen leaving with her. He chuckled when he thought about it being licensed in California to one of Pit Bull's aliases. *If they ever tracked Bull down … that would be a real hoot.*

Rolling to a stop at the end of the dirt road, Richard cut the engine. He sighed in relief. So far his plan was working.

Inside the trailer, he turned on the small air-conditioning unit in the bedroom, fluffed up the pillow on the bed, and walked out to get Victoria. Still unconscious, he carefully pulled her from the vehicle, shut the door with his foot, and carried her to the bed in the trailer.

He wasn't sure how long she would be out—probably not much longer. It didn't matter if she came to now or later, he had to remove the license plate, swapping the car with one he rented the day before he rented the trailer. He checked the gag over her mouth, then the cord around her wrists and ankles.

He sat on the bed next to her unconscious body. "Victoria, I hope to God you can forgive me for luring ... I had to," he whispered. "I won't hurt you. I promise I won't hurt you. Just a couple of days ... if you want to leave you can."

Standing up, he released a heavy sigh, then hurried out of the trailer locking the door as he left.

Retracing the route he had just taken as far as I-95, he turned into the Super Wal-Mart lot and parked in the far corner shielded by a group of trees. He locked the car, threw the keys into a trash can as he strolled by, entered the main entrance and out through the garden center gate.

He trotted to the back of the parking lot on the opposite side of the store bordered with large palmetto bushes. Unlocking the gray sedan he had parked earlier in the day, he slid behind the wheel and drove off to rejoin Victoria. The round trip took him less than an hour.

Clouds were forming in the west. He felt a humid breeze as he unlocked the trailer. Sticking his head through the bedroom door, it appeared that Victoria was still sleeping so he fetched a can of beer from the fridge, walked back to the bedroom and sat down. Taking a swig, he looked at her face and noticed her eyelids flutter.

Victoria's eyes opened wide, filled with fear, as she struggled against her restraints to no avail, her voice muffled by the gag.

"Victoria, I'm sorry, but you gave me no choice. If I take off the gag do you promise you won't scream?"

She nodded, yes.

"Promise?"

She nodded again.

Setting his beer down on the floor, he carefully untied the blue-silk scarf and laid it on the bedside table.

"What the hell do you think you're doing?" she yelled.

"I said no screaming or the gag goes back," he said glaring at her as he sat back down. Picking up his beer, he took a long swig, wiped his mouth with his hand, and continued to stare at her. "You suggested we talk tomorrow," he said. "Well, it's tomorrow."

"What?"

"No, no. You haven't slept that long—under two hours."

"Slept?" she yelled. "You knocked me out. You kidnapped me. Kidnapped! You can go to jail for that," she snapped. "Kelly? Oh my God. Is Kelly all right? I swear to God if you hurt her I'll scratch your eyes out."

"Kelly's fine. Let's just say I borrowed you."

"Why? What do you want?" she snapped.

"Money."

"This is about my husband isn't it?"

Careful, Razor. Don't tip your hand ... don't show her you care. This job is your future, if you have a future. Goof up and Bull will put a bullet in your head. It depends on her cooperation. He stood. Took a step toward the bed, he could at least untie her ankles. "NO," he yelled, clenching his fists at the ceiling. *Get out of the room. Get away from her.*

Victoria jerked on the bed, fearing he was going to hit her. Instead he turned abruptly, leaving her, slamming the bedroom door behind him, storming out of the trailer. He ran down to the river flowing along the edge of the property. "Get a hold of yourself, Robert Steele," he cried out, tramping onto the dock. Slowly he brought his breathing under control. He walked back up the path to the trailer and seconds later reentered the bedroom.

"Quick aren't you?" he said in an icy tone. "Yes, this is about your husband. I always thought you were a smart woman. The next few days we'll see just how smart you really are. Play along with me and you won't get hurt."

Victoria's tone changed ... softened. "Richard, I know you won't hurt me ... I don't know who you are, but the other Richard said he loved me and I believe him."

Razor stared at her. "Don't test me, Mrs. Brookfield." His voice was cold, the menacing words lingering in the air as he untied her wrists and ankles. Then he strode out of the bedroom door and locked it.

Chapter 22

—

WIND GUSTS, RAIN CLOUDS, and sporadic lightning rolled in from the west as Harri Brookfield dashed into the mall. Weaving in and out the early-evening shoppers he spotted his daughter pacing in front of Macy's entrance.

"Kelly," he shouted. Her body language told him she had not seen her mother. She looked frightened running into the safety of his arms.

Unable to hold the tears back, she buried her head in his chest. "Daddy, something awful has happened. I know it has. What are we going to do?" She looked up to him for an answer, tears trickling down her cheeks.

"How long has it been since you saw her?" he asked still holding her in his protective arms.

Stepping back, she looked around. "I got to the mall about 4:30 and mom was sitting at that little table over there." Kelly pointed to the black-iron table where a mother and her young son were enjoying a burger.

Harri looked at his watch. "After seven, so it's been more than two hours. Let's go home. Show me where your car's parked." Harri guided Kelly through the crowd, a firm grip on her elbow as he propelled her forward. Outside the mall, they half walked and half ran to her car. Fumbling with her keys, Harri took them from her trembling fingers, clicked the button to release the door locks, and walked Kelly to the passenger side. "I'll drive us to my car then you drive your car. I'll follow you home. Are you okay to drive?"

"Yes. I'll be okay," she said sliding into the car and regaining some of her composure now that her dad was with her.

"I'm going to call Polly again," Kelly said, punching in her number. "Maybe mom's called her." Polly answered on the first ring. "Polly, did … no? Okay, Dad and I are headed home. … A detective? … let me ask him." Kelly turned to her father. "Polly says she knows a detective who's done some work for her. She said you and mom met her at a party. Okay if she brings her over to talk to us? Maybe she can help."

"Tell her yes. We need help." Harri's grip tightened around the steering wheel.

Chapter 23

July 12, Monday, 7:30 P.M.

TURNING INTO HIS DRIVEWAY Harri triggered the garage door opener and rolled in. Vicky's car was not on the other side of the garage. Kelly followed, parking in the driveway as Harri hurried into the kitchen, Kelly on his heels. Striding to the phone, he picked up the receiver and tried once again to reach Vicky's cell at the same time the doorbell rang.

"I'll get it, Dad. It's probably Polly," Kelly said, striding to the front door.

Kelly opened the door and Polly stepped inside, gave Kelly a quick hug, and then introduced her to Elizabeth Stitchway.

"Miss Stitchway, I'm glad you came. Dad's in the kitchen."

Polly and Liz followed Kelly down the hall and saw Harri bang down the kitchen phone.

Vicky did not answer.

The sun retreating for the day caused the stark white kitchen to fade into the dim gray of evening.

"Hello, Mr. Brookfield," Liz said extending her hand.

"Thanks for coming, Elizabeth. Please everyone have a seat," Harri said. He looked back at the phone hanging on the wall, worry lines creasing his face.

"Mr. Brookfield—"

"Harri."

"Harri, tell me why you think your wife is missing and not simply shopping?" Liz asked. "Polly indicated that it's only been a couple of hours since—"

"I'm not sure," Harri cut in. "But I am concerned. It's not like Vicky. We both try to keep in touch ... I." Harri looked at his daughter, then stood, took a few steps, rubbed his forehead and turned back to Liz. "Yes, I think something's happened to her."

"Okay, then call the police. Ask for Captain Manny Salinas. Here's the number." Liz retrieved one of her new business cards, jotted down the Daytona Beach Police Department number on the back and handed it to him.

The three women held Harri in their eyes as he punched in the number and asked for Captain Salinas.

"He's gone for the day? … this is an emergency … my wife's missing. Please, find the Captain and put me through to him! Okay. Ask him to call me at … you have it? Ask him to call immediately."

Harri slapped the phone into the wall cradle. Clinging to it, his head bent down. The silence was broken with the ring of the phone.

"Brookfield. … Captain? … A Miss Stitchway is here at my house. She said to call you … my wife's missing … yes, please come over." Harri gave the captain the address and hung up.

———

WITHIN TEN MINUTES A black SUV pulled into the Brookfield driveway and parked. The lace curtain covering Mildred's window parted slightly from the frame as a stocky man with black hair and moustache, dressed all in black, strode to the front door and was invited inside before he had a chance to ring the doorbell.

"Mr. Brookfield?"

Harri nodded extending his hand. "Thanks for coming so quickly, Captain. We're in the kitchen." Harri led the way then stepped to the side.

"Captain, this is my daughter Kelly, my neighbor Polly Pringle and her friend, a private investigator, Elizabeth Stitchway."

Manny nodded to Kelly and Polly and then turned to Liz. "When you called for information the other day, I didn't get a chance to tell you that I heard you were back in town," Manny said his eyes puzzled, wondering how it was that Liz was in the Brookfield kitchen.

Liz stood up and shook Manny's outstretched hand.

"Manny. Nice to see you," she said pulling her hand from his warm grip. "I moved back a couple of months ago. Polly asked me to come over. See if I could help her neighbor. Mr. Brookfield is so certain his wife is missing that I suggested he call you." Liz smiled their eyes locking for a brief moment.

Liz sat down as Harri drew up a chair for Captain Salinas but they both remained standing.

"Mr. Brookfield, when did you last see your wife?"

"This morning, but Kelly met her at the mall this afternoon. Kelly, tell the captain what happened." He and Manny sat down, drawing closer to Kelly.

"There really isn't much to tell. I had an interview at Halifax Hospital. Mom and I were going to go shopping when I was done. I called to tell her I was on my way and she said to meet her in front of Macy's. When I got there she was sitting at a little table by the coffee shop just before the entrance to Macy's. She wanted a glass of iced coffee and I said I'd hold the table. She never returned. I looked in the store and when I couldn't find her I called dad. While I waited for him, I called Polly, she lives next door—oh, dad already told you that. Anyway, I was checking if mom had called her. Dad met me in front of Macy's." Kelly stopped, her hands clasped tightly together in her lap.

"Did you see your mother buy the coffee?" Manny asked.

"Well, no. I was texting my friend, Carol. She wanted to know about the interview and then she told me about a date she had with her new boyfriend, and ... oh, Miss Stitchway. I was so intent on talking to Carol that when I looked at the time, well, mom had been gone for over thirty minutes ... almost an hour." Tears began to fill Kelly's frightened eyes. "Oh, Daddy, it's all my fault. I wasn't paying attention, I never looked up, I—"

"That was one of the first things that nice Detective Miles told my self-defense class."

"What was that Polly," Liz asked.

"Be aware of your surroundings at all times."

"Do you think she's okay, Captain," Kelly asked, wadding up her father's handkerchief he had tucked in her hand, dabbing her eyes.

"Let's hope so, Kelly. We'll do our best to find her. Mr. Brookfield, are you sure she just didn't meet a friend, or maybe there was a medical problem—she became confused?"

Harri didn't answer. He stood up, his chair grating on the tile floor as he pushed back. He rubbed his temple and then turned to Polly.

"Thanks, Polly, for your help. I'll fill the captain in about Vicky." Harri walked to the back door and opened it. "We'll call you if we hear anything."

Polly, flustered at being excused, got the hint and left saying goodbye to Kelly and Liz on her way out. Liz and Manny exchanged a quick glance at Brookfield's abrupt dismissal of his neighbor, and Kelly sat wide-eyed witnessing her father's rude behavior.

Manny broke the silence as Harri stood staring at the closed door. "Is there something you want to say, Mr. Brookfield?"

Harri walked slowly back to the kitchen table, took hold of the back of his chair, and looked at his precious daughter, pain in his eyes.

"Kelly, I have something to tell you. I need your understanding. You're only sixteen … your mother and I had hoped this day would never come, but apparently … I hope to God I'm wrong … but … I'm afraid I'm not. You have to be told."

"Daddy, you're scaring me," Kelly whispered clutching the damp handkerchief.

"I'm sorry. I don't mean to." Harri walked to the sink, gripped the edge, head down. He looked up, out the window. Taking a deep breath, he straightened his body to its full five-foot-eleven height and turned to the three people watching him. Waiting.

"Captain Salinas, my name is Herbert Babcock. People want to kill me, stop me from testifying against the man I saw kill my business partner. I witnessed the murder. The only way the Feds felt I could live to give that testimony was if they put my wife and I … and Kelly, in their witness protection program. Eleven years ago we were relocated here. Daytona Beach. The murderer has never been caught. The case is open. I'm still waiting to testify. It appears that those who want to kill me have found me and have taken my wife."

Chapter 24

—

July 12, Monday, 9:01 P.M.

SILENCE AND DARK SHADOWS of night filled the Brookfield's sterile, white kitchen. Harri turned on the small light fixture hanging over the table casting sharp shadows into the corners of the room. Kelly drew the blinds covering the black glass and then put on a pot of coffee. Her father had a story to tell. She could feel the responsibility of adulthood creeping into her bones—her youth was about to end.

Manny broke the silence.

"Harri, I think you'd better tell us more about why you're in the witness protection program and why you think your past has something to do with your wife's disappearance today."

Harri stood, took a couple of steps, hands on his hips, and stared into space, thinking. Kelly removed four mugs from the cupboard setting them on the counter. She didn't look at the others—she needed a few minutes to brace herself for what was to come.

The sound from percolating coffee stopped. Liz got up to help her new, young friend. She poured the coffee, setting a mug at each place while Kelly put out the spoons, sugar bowl, and a pitcher of half-and-half. She sat down and looked at her father, the captain's request for more information still hanging in the air.

"Okay, Dad, tell me what happened when I was five years old."

"As you know, Kelly, I write computer code, programs, and design hardware, mainly computer chips. By the time I graduated from college, I had drawn up a design for a super chip. Cell phones were the rage, but they were big and clumsy. Email had been around for a long time on the internet. My design had the potential to speed up all the wireless communications that were coming. A friend, Frank Pitman, a guy I went to school with at Stanford and a fellow computer science student, said we should hook up, go into partnership, that he knew a couple of venture capitalists who would back us. We did just that—we formed a legal partnership."

"Where was this partnership located?" Manny asked, looking up from the notes he had taken on a yellow pad of paper.

"San Francisco." Harri paused taking a sip of coffee. As he told his story, his head swam with questions—how was he going to escape from being killed this time? He supposed WITSEC would relocate the family again. A marshal could charge through the door and whisk them away, no questions asked, once he called.

"Frank handled the financial side of the business. I never met the man who finally put up the money. I was only twenty-four, newly married, stars in my eyes with the possibility of starting my own company with Frank—partners."

"You and mom were young when you got married," Kelly mumbled, looking down at the table.

"Yes, young, and very much in love. She …" Harri looked up at the ceiling then back to Kelly. He took another sip of his black coffee, inhaled a deep breath and slowly exhaled.

"A year into the business, we were suddenly bombarded by several high-tech firms that wanted to buy our designs. A bidding war broke out. But I knew the designs weren't ready. There were flaws that had to be addressed. However, Frank insisted we take the highest offer. Make a killing while we could. Everything was happening so fast in the industry—mergers and acquisitions were rampant—firms buying companies they thought would catapult them ahead of their competitors. They were paying huge sums for designs that filled a hole in their product lines. We were offered ten million dollars to buy us out. Kelly, have you heard the term whistleblower?"

"Yes, someone who makes public, something that's dishonest."

"That's right. And many times the whistleblower faces reprisals by the people he accused of doing something dishonest."

"Is that what you did, Dad? You blew the whistle on your partner?"

"Yes. But what I was unaware of at the time was that the venture capitalist, who invested the initial million dollars, and triple that amount to move us into a swanky office building with our team, was a drug dealer. He always looked to make a quick return on his investments—be it drugs or computer designs. We were a front for his operation. He used us to launder his dirty money. Unfortunately, Frank confided all this to me after I blew the whistle. Everything came to light—the design flaws, the drug money, the laundering and the fact that the investor was part of a large cartel from Mexico. He also wanted his cut, half of the sale of the company. I was now the star witness in fraud with a drug connection, and very much a liability to Frank and his dirty pals. If the sale didn't go through then there was no ten million dollars."

"That's when the feds stepped in to protect their star witness—you?" Manny said. He walked over to the coffeepot and, with a nod to each asking if they wanted a refill, topped off their coffee.

"No. Not yet. It got worse," Harri said. "I saw a man shoot Pitman, a shot that was intended for me. I fell to the floor next to Frank and the shooter fled. But I saw his face. His pudgy face is seared into my brain—his eyes. Eyes full of hate. Evil. After he fled, the police tried to blame another man, a man I had never seen before. I said, no, and the evidence didn't support their theory. The manhunt for the killer of my partner lasted several years, and then I guess they lost interest in the case. They never found him."

Sitting down, Manny picked up his pen, jotted down a few words, and looked up at Harri. "What's the name of the U.S. Marshal assigned to your case? I'm obligated to call him, to fill him in on the situation. I guess you're supposed to do that, too. Have you?"

"Not yet, but I will tonight. His name is Ken Fisher." Harri dug into his jeans pocket for his wallet. Poking around in the sleeves of the billfold, he retrieved a worn scrap of paper and pushed it in front of Manny. Manny wrote the telephone number on his pad and pushed the scrap back to Harri.

"Why is a name scratched out? This Fisher is written above," Manny asked.

"My original handler called a while back. He was being reassigned but he thought Fisher was taking over even though the case was old."

"I need a recent picture of your wife and a description of what she was wearing the last time you saw her. I guess, Kelly, that would be you," Manny said.

Kelly jumped up from her chair, palms flat on the table, and looked straight at her father. There was no smile on her face. "What about my grandparents. I kept asking about them but you always put me off. Why didn't they visit? Don't they care about me? You and mom told me her parents are in France and yours are in Alaska. Is that where they really live?"

"No," Harri whispered looking straight back at his daughter. "They're in San Francisco."

"Yours and mom's?"

"Yes."

"How long?"

"Eleven years."

"I want to see them," Kelly said her palms still on the table.

"You can't."

"You can't. Is that what you said to mom—you can't? Maybe she did run away."

"Kelly, I—"

"Excuse me," Kelly snapped. "I have to print a picture. I took one with my cell a few weeks ago at the last quilter's meeting. Will that be okay, Captain Salinas?" Kelly continued to stare at her father.

"Sounds good. How many were at this meeting or club?" Manny asked trying to defuse the bitterness he saw on Kelly's face.

"There were five of us—four in the picture. It was at Polly's house."

"Don't cut the other ladies out. Give me the whole photo."

"Kelly, print two copies, please. I'd like one as well," Liz said.

"Sure. Be right back." Kelly stood up, turned away from her father, and marched out of the kitchen.

"I'm sorry, Harri," Manny said. "I can't imagine how difficult this must be for you. I have a few more questions while she gets the picture and then I'll be leaving. Give me a description of Mrs. Brookfield—height, weight, eye and hair color."

Harri stood, paced around the room, answering Manny's questions about his wife as Manny and Liz took notes. Kelly returned handing a copy of the picture to her dad, raised her eyebrow for his okay. He nodded and she handed a copy to Manny and one to Liz.

"Thanks, Kelly. Have you heard about the 48-hour rule?" Manny asked.

"No. What's that?"

"Well, people have a tendency to forget things as time passes," Manny said. "That's why I wanted to talk to you tonight, while what you saw is fresh in your mind. Did you see anything unusual at the mall, was your mother herself or did she appear fearful—looking around as if someone had bothered her?"

"Oh, no. She wanted to hear about the interview and that's why she suggested we have coffee before shopping." The tension a few minutes earlier had eased. Kelly glanced at her father, sighed, as her shoulders drooped.

"Tell me what your mother was wearing—everything tip to toe, colors, and fabric," Manny said.

Kelly closed her eyes visualizing her mother. "She had on a brown T-shirt, dark brown, stretch cotton. White capris, and brown sandals. The sandals were jeweled. Her shoulder bag was white."

Manny wrote down Vicky's description and returned the pad to his pocket. "I'll be in touch with your marshal to see how he wants to handle this missing-person search. "I'm sure he won't want us to put out an APB on your wife or flash her picture on television or the internet, in case what you suspect is true. However, I will get Mrs. Brookfield's description out to my men in the field tonight. You never know—one of them could spot her."

"If you don't need me, Captain, I'd like to go to my room," Kelly said.

"That's it for now, Kelly. Thanks for your help—call me anytime if you think of something that might shine some light on what happened."

Liz glanced at her watch. It was after ten. The tension had taken a toll on everyone's nerves.

"Harri, I'd like you to come over to my office tomorrow," Manny said. "We can set a time after I talk to Fisher. I may call you again tonight. Here's my card with my direct line and cell numbers."

"Okay, Captain."

"How about you call me Manny. I have a feeling we're going to be seeing a lot of each other. Liz, I'd like to talk to you in the morning. Can you swing by around eight?"

"Of course. I'll be leaving in a few minutes. I want to say goodnight to Kelly."

Manny glanced quickly at Liz, his brows slightly furrowed.

"Don't worry, I'll tell you if we come up with any new information. But right now, she's a scared little girl—it doesn't matter how old she is. By the way, I met Mrs. Brookfield at Joe Rocket's party—where I met Polly."

"I see. I'm going back to the department and get this picture out to the field."

Manny stood and shook Harri's hand. He turned to leave but stopped and looked back at Harri.

"You understand, she may not have been kidnapped. Mrs. Brookfield might have run away."

Chapter 25

July 12, Monday, 10:05 P.M.

THE BLACK SUV BACKED out of the Brookfield driveway and sped away into the humid, inky-black night. Manny's statement that there was a possibility Vicky ran away, as he walked out the door, swept over Harri and Kelly when the captain excused himself to initiate the investigation. Harri returned to the kitchen to find Kelly leaning forward, elbows on the table, talking to Liz.

"Kelly, does your mom use a computer?"

"Yes. Mostly for email but I know she looks up information, especially on artists. She's collected books on Monet, Van Gogh—"

"I'd like to take a look on the computer she uses. I'm sure Manny will be sending a detective over to check it for clues—who she's been emailing. I'd like your mom's email address."

Liz pushed the tablet to her and a pen.

"Kelly, please call me Liz. Do you know your mom's password?"

"Yes. I helped her set up the account."

"Harri, do you mind if I take a look at her account? It may give us some information. Maybe she asked a friend to join her and Kelly at the mall today."

"No, I don't mind. Anything you can do."

"Do you and your wife use the same computer?"

"No. I'm usually at work, but I do have a laptop that I cart around. Kelly, take Liz to the study while I put on another pot of coffee."

The Brookfield study was like the rest of the house—white, sterile. It was homey but in a store display sort of way. No pictures, No knickknacks. Nothing personal.

Kelly started the computer and Liz sat down in front of the monitor. The screen of the desktop appeared and Liz clicked on the internet explorer icon. "What email service do you use, Kelly?"

"Hotmail. Both mom and I. Dad uses Yahoo."

Liz opened the Hotmail login screen and typed in Vicky's username and password. Her inbox contained eighteen messages. Except for the fact most of the messages were marked as read, it appeared Vicky kept a clean inbox—filing or deleting messages as a regular routine. The most current message, time-stamped twenty minutes ago, was a sales advertisement from Coldwater Creek. Liz clicked on the Sent folder and found it empty. Vicky had set up a few folders and one caught Liz's eye. Clicking on the folder, Liz asked, "Who's Richard?"

Kelly pulled up a chair beside Liz. Harri had joined them and was reading the screen over Liz's shoulder.

"I don't know," Kelly said. "She never mentioned that name to me."

"How about you, Harri? Do you know a Richard?"

"No, she never mentioned the name to me either."

"Well, these emails start over two months ago."

"Open them, Liz," Harri said lowering his head so he could see better.

"Okay, let's start down here in the list." Liz opened several messages, each seemed to deal with setting up a time and place to meet for coffee or lunch. She clicked to open one dated in the first week of June. "Oh, oh. Take a look at this, Harri."

"Dear Richard, yesterday was wonderful—talking to someone who actually listened to me. For the first time in years I felt alive. My marriage has been under a terrible strain—I don't know who I am any more. I feel like I'm in a prison. In answer to your question—yes I want to see you again."

A tear trickled down Kelly's check and Liz grasped her hand. "Liz, does this mean mom was having an affair?"

"He could just be a very good friend, but they were seeing each other quite a bit by the looks of these emails," Liz replied as she continued to read the messages.

Harri slumped into an easy chair next to the desk. Setting his coffee on the end table, he laid his head back and looked up at the ceiling.

"I know our life was hard for her. She never adjusted to the circumstances we found ourselves in. Leaving her friends, family, especially her mother. I'm gone a lot … at work, but—" He stood up, yanked his hair tight through the elastic holding his ponytail. "Kelly, I had to work long hours—after all, we needed things—I had to provide for you."

Kelly looked at her father, suddenly defensive, seeking her approval. She turned away … looking back at the computer screen.

"This is odd," Liz said.

"What's odd?" Harri said with irritation in his voice.

"Richard, whoever he is, used one of those email accounts that you buy to create an alias. You can activate it for a few hours, days or a longer period of time. People use this service for their business or sometimes to hide their identity. Do you mind if I forward this to Manny and myself so we can trace it?"

"No, please, go ahead." Harri was once again standing behind Liz. "Do you think it will help us find Vicky?"

"I don't know, but it's strange. I'm going to forward all of these messages. The folder shows more than fifty over a two-month period."

Liz turned and faced Harri. "Maybe Captain Salinas was right—your wife ran away. Ran away with this Richard person."

Chapter 26

—

LIZ SLEPT FITFULLY—jumping out of bed every hour, traipsing to the computer with another thought on how to find Mrs. Brookfield. Her dog Maggie finally gave up following her back and forth and fell asleep on the rug by the computer.

At 7:15 in the morning Liz hurried up to the Brookfield front door and rang the bell. Harri was expecting her. She had called him twenty minutes earlier saying she had to see him.

"Good morning, Harri. How's Kelly doing?" Liz asked stepping into the house. She noted the circles under Harri's eyes and the stubble on his chin. His ponytail was askew.

"I'm not sure. That was a lot of information thrown at her last night on top of her mother's gone missing," he said.

"Is she here? I want to show you something on the computer and I'd like Kelly to be with us."

Harri led the way to the study his flip-flops clicking on the tile floor. He poked his head into his daughter's room on the way.

"Kelly, Liz is here—come join us in the study as soon as you can, honey."

Harri and Liz continued down the hall to the study. He turned on the computer and just as the desktop icons appeared Kelly entered the room in her pajamas.

"Hi. Did you get any sleep last night?" Liz asked giving the girl a quick hug hoping to provide her a little comfort.

"Some. I'm skipping class today—I want to be here in case mom calls.

Liz again sat at the computer, opened the internet browser and logged into her FaceBook account. Clicking in the search box, she typed Kelly's first and last name. Kelly's latest post immediately filled the screen. She hadn't posted anything new since the time she began looking for her mother at Macy's.

Scrolling down to the post Kelly had entered before her interview at the hospital, she looked up at Kelly. "Okay, first, as far as FaceBook is concerned, you and I are not friends but I can see your posts."

"Right, I could ask you to be a friend, or you could ask me, and we would have to answer one way or the other," Kelly said.

"But, I can see your post. Your FaceBook account must be set so everyone can see what you type—we aren't friends but I can see your entry. Here, let me show you. I'm logged into my account. My setting is *friends only*. See that?" Liz pointed to the setting displayed on her account profile and looked up at Kelly and then to Harri standing behind her.

"Now, I'll post a note on my wall." Liz typed, "Looks like another beautiful day in Florida." She then logged out of her account, switched seats with Kelly and asked her to log into her FaceBook account. Liz instructed her to search for Elizabeth Stitchway. The program responded that it found the name and asked if she wanted to send an invitation to be her friend.

"Don't answer that at the moment, Kelly. Just understand that you can't see the words I posted a few minutes ago—*you're not my friend*. My account is set so only people who can see my posts must be *my friends*. Now scroll down to that posting of yours I found when I was logged into my account."

"There it is," Kelly said.

"Please read it to your dad."

"About to have an interview for a part-time job after school this fall. Wish me luck. Then Mom and I are going shopping at Macy's and out to dinner."

"Now, Kelly," Liz said, "click on your account settings and look at who has the privilege of seeing your postings."

"Everyone."

"Not good! I have another warning for you and I'm sure you've heard it before," Liz said.

"What's that?" Kelly asked.

"Anything you type, or upload onto the internet—whether it's FaceBook, your emails, websites … anywhere, anything—will be out there forever. You intend what you type for a particular person or persons, but that someone can send it on to someone else, who sends it to someone else … on and on. FaceBook, in Twitter, your personal email accounts are wonderful tools but they can also result in great personal pain and embarrassment for *all* the years of your life and beyond. These applications are not the cause of trouble—we, the users, are. Whatever you put on the internet has eternal life. Do you understand what I'm saying?"

"Oh, yes. The Human Resource lady, who interviewed me, had looked me up on FaceBook. It wasn't what I said that she commented on but the volume of posts."

"Okay, log out. Harri, can we go to the kitchen?" Liz asked backing away from the computer.

"Sure," Harri said, his face grim.

Walking down the hall, Liz saw a bedroom she hadn't noticed before. It was beautiful—pale blue walls, lace and ribbon pillow shams on a matching quilt. There was a picture of an older couple on the nightstand. This room was decorated by a woman with a flair for design—a stark contrast to the rest of the rooms she had seen in the house.

"Coffee, Liz? I put on a fresh pot after you called," Harri said.

"Yes, please." Liz sat in the same chair as the night before, while Kelly put out the cream and sugar. "Mulling over everything that was said last night, I came up with a couple of assumptions."

Harri placed a mug of steaming coffee in front of Liz and sat down opposite her, taking a sip from his mug. "Tell us what you're thinking."

"First. Let's say someone with a grudge against you is lurking around the net trying to find you, or more to the point, knows where you are, but is looking for an opportunity."

"An opportunity to do what?" Kelly asked, pouring herself a glass of milk and then taking a seat at the table.

"To carry out this grudge—by kidnapping your mother."

"Oh no," Kelly whispered her hand covering her mouth, eyes squeezed shut.

"Remember, this is just an assumption. But after what your father told us last night, we have to assume it's a possibility except it could be way more than a grudge. So he could be a she, reads Kelly's post and sees it as an opportunity."

"But, Liz, Vicky didn't scream or someone would have come to help. There must have been a lot of people around her at that time of day, and Kelly didn't—"

"I know. Kelly didn't hear a scream or see anything that would have alarmed her."

"It's all my fault. I was talking to Carol—I wasn't watching—"

"Hey, hey, Kelly. It's not your fault. If Liz's assumption is even remotely on the mark, this bad person would have found me another way."

"Second. As you said, Harri, Mrs. Brookfield didn't scream, at least not at that moment when she was buying the coffees, so maybe someone lured her away, out of the mall. Someone she knew."

"Maybe that Richard person." Harri spit out the name. "Liz, I want you to help us. Will you?"

"I'm on my way to see Captain Salinas. Maybe he's made contact with the marshal—see how Fisher wants to handle Mrs. Brookfield's disappearance. I'll let you know this afternoon. Sometimes the police don't like it when someone outside the department gets involved. Of course, I did meet you and Mrs. Brookfield at Rocket's party."

Chapter 27

THE DESK SERGEANT NOTIFIED Captain Salinas that a Miss Stitchway was in the lobby with her dog and what did he want to do about it?

"Tell her I'll be right down. We'll go into Conference Room A."

Liz turned away from the desk sergeant sitting behind bullet-proof glass and looked out the large, floor-to-ceiling, bullet-proof window. A fortress. Maggie, her black and white Border collie tethered by a leash, kept pace. At a pinging sound, the elevator door slid open and Peaches, Manny's black Labrador, bounded out to greet Maggie. The dogs, both rescued from a shelter, circled each other as Manny walked up to Liz ready to give his friend a peck on the cheek. Liz had her hand out, but noting a peck was coming her way, leaned in as Manny pulled back seeing her hand and extended his, resulting in a slight punch to her stomach. Both chuckled in embarrassment, the dogs watching the antics of their respective owners. Manny cut into the embarrassing silence. "Thanks for coming over, Stitch. The conference room is right over here. Glad to see you still have Maggie. When you moved to Ocala, I swear Peaches was in a funk for weeks." Liz relaxed—they were back on friendly terms—Manny and Stitch.

Manny led the way followed by Peaches, then Liz and Maggie. Taking seats on opposite sides of the table, their dogs immediately laid down to the right of their masters' chairs. Liz pulled a pad from her briefcase and Manny laid his yellow pad on the table. They both wore black from head to toe—if not in the police station, they could be perceived as ready for a major jewelry heist.

Manny was the first to speak. "As I said last night, I heard you were back in town. Did you close your office in Ocala?"

"Yes. There wasn't enough business, plus I know more people here. I rented a vacant space in a little strip mall on Nova Road in Port Orange."

"Which one?" Manny asked, a warm smile crossing his face, his dark eyes taking in her red hair, changed to a glowing auburn framing her large brown eyes.

"By the Pennysaver newspaper office and Gaff's Meats."

"Oh, yea. Maybe Peaches and I will run into you some morning—at the meat market. They have great dog bones."

"Maybe." Liz flashed a tentative smile and looked down at her notepad. "I stopped by Brookfield's this morning."

"Liz, we have to—"

"I know. I know. It's essentially a police matter."

"How did you happen to be there last night … besides knowing the neighbor?"

"The neighbor you met, Polly, is a client of mine. She and I were at a party that Rocket, Joe Rockwell, threw for his clients— remember him?"

"The ex-con. You helped to clear him."

"Manny, he was acquitted of all charges *and* he was paid restitution for the three years of his life when he was erroneously incarcerated," Liz said trying to keep the irritation out of her voice— unsuccessfully. "Anyway, Brookfield asked me to work for him. Did you talk to the marshal?"

"Wait. Backup." Manny said.

Hearing the gruffness in his voice, she tensed for what she expected was not to *back up* but to *back off*.

"Brookfield's missing wife could wrap up quickly or it could drag on," Manny said. "I'm shorthanded and you just opened an office. It can take time for a new PI to gather enough clients to pay the office rent, not to mention a house mortgage … so, I'm offering you a few billable hours on this case."

Liz jumped up from her chair, hands on her hips. "Hey, don't think you have to throw me a bone," she shot back.

"You redheads are all alike—offer you a job and you fly off the handle. Go figure."

"My hair color is none of your business. Offer me a job with a stated number of hours per week, on this case, the Brookfield missing-wife case, and I'll take it." Liz was marching around the table but ended her statement with an I-dare-you stare.

"Okay. Ten hours over the next week. You give me what you find and when you hit ten hours … on an itemized timesheet … we'll see where the case stands."

Liz sighed. She knew he had her. She needed the money and even though her former boss, Goodwurthy PI Services, said he would give her some business, he hadn't exactly burned up the telephone line to her office.

"I accept." Liz sat down and flipped to the notes she had taken this morning. Her head snapped up. "But, I'll also accept Brookfield's offer."

"Wait—"

"Don't worry, I won't double dip. When your hours are reached on any given week, I'll charge my time over that to Brookfield. However, to show my good faith … and integrity, I'll let you know what I'm doing, on his case, on his clock." She gave a sharp nod of her head as a punctuation mark.

"Okay, but I said ten hours this week and then we see where the case stands. Okay?"

"Okay!"

"So," Manny said, letting out a sigh, "what did you find out this morning?"

"Last night Brookfield seemed to think there was a connection with his past and his missing wife. So I started thinking about different scenarios. By the way, I'm considering this conversation with you to be on the clock."

"Fine, but starting now. When you accepted. Not last night … or your meeting this morning with Brookfield."

Liz shot Manny a snarly look and continued. "When Kelly was waiting for her mother to bring the coffees, there was no disturbance. So maybe Vicky saw someone she knew and left with that person. But who?"

"Did you find anything on the computer?"

"Yes, a man named Richard and …," Liz paused keeping him hanging. He nodded with raised eyebrows for her to continue.

"And the fact that Kelly had posted a note on her FaceBook page that she and her mom would meet at Macy's and the appointed time."

"So you were the one who asked Kelly to forward me those messages between Vicky and the man named Richard."

"Did you read them?"

"Yes. Nothing like corresponding by email to jumpstart a relationship on the fast track to love and romance. It amazes me how quickly people become intimate after a few emails. In this case, it seems they met after several emails and the new relationship became hot. Very hot."

"Exactly, although I've only read a couple. I'm sure you noted that Kelly sent me copies as well?" Liz asked. This time her eyebrows shot up.

"So noted."

"Good." Liz leaned over and gave Maggie a pat.

Manny didn't realize he did the same—patting Peaches on her silky head. Peaches leaned into Manny's hand, loving the attention.

"Now," Liz said, "what did the marshal have to say about Brookfield, aka Babcock?"

"Fisher's based in Orlando which leads me to believe he has others around central Florida in the WITSEC program. He was skeptical that the disappearance of Brookfield's wife had something to do with the eleven-year-old case. Anyway, he said he'd check if there was anything new with the players involved, and he is definitely going to visit Harri Brookfield."

Chapter 28

———

July 13, Tuesday, 10:16 A.M.

VICTORIA PACED THE TRAILER'S tiny bedroom—her prison cell. If she thought she was a prisoner before, she now realized the fallacy of those thoughts. The room was paneled with fake wood, smelled musty, and the humidity coupled with the lack of ventilation dampened the bedcovers.

Looking out the one small window, she saw that the trailer sat no more than a few yards from some water. Because of the thick growth of pine trees, she could only see a small section of the water and couldn't tell if it was a lake or a river. There was a dock about fifteen feet long. A rowboat was tied to it. Thick clouds covered the sun. She was certain it was still morning—maybe nine or eleven—but there was no way to tell exactly.

"Victoria, are you decent?" Richard called through the door.

"What do you care?" she yelled back.

She heard a key inserted into a lock but the door had no keyhole. *He must have installed a padlock on the other side,* she thought. The door swung open and there he stood, his solid frame filling the doorway. He had a cup of a coffee in one hand, a small paper bag in the other, and a box tucked under his arm. The scowl on his face made her back away stumbling against the only chair in the room. She hated herself for ever thinking she loved him. She didn't know this Richard who walked toward her.

"Sit down. Don't move out of the chair," he said in a low, controlled voice. He put the box on the bed, the coffee and the bag on the bedside table. He swung around grabbing a chair he had dragged from the other side of the door. He put the chair in the doorway facing her but continued to stand behind it.

"Get your coffee. There's a bagel in the sack. Then go back and sit in the chair. We need to talk."

She did as she was told. Taking the bagel out of the bag she noticed he had included two creamers. Coffee the way she liked it. This was from the Richard who said he loved her.

"I have to make a call. A call to Herbert Babcock. Know him?"

Victoria's head snapped up at the name, a veil of fear fell over her face.

"You know he's my husband," she whispered.

"Yes, I do. I just wanted to be sure you remembered. Last night I told you if you follow my instructions nothing will happen to you ... or to Mr. Babcock. But if you try to get away before my little deal with your husband is complete, then both of you will be killed. You know there's a price on his head?"

"I hoped after eleven years it was over."

"Oh, come on, Victoria. You know the case is still open. Your husband could still testify if, a *big if,* he's alive. Now ... I'm going to call your husband. He may ask to talk to you. Verify you're all right. However, the call is going to be very short so he really won't have a chance to ask about his precious, adulterous wife."

Victoria closed her eyes, her head dropping forward. If the cruel words, dripping with venom, were meant to slice through her heart he succeeded.

"Go ahead and enjoy your coffee, Victoria, while I have a little chat with your husband." He pulled a cell from his pants pocket, punched in the number saying each as he did so. There was no doubt who he was calling.

The phone was picked up on the first ring.

"Mr. Babcock?"

"Who's this?"

"I have your wife. Now listen good. You will wire two million dollars to a bank in return for your wife. The money will be wired in two days. You will receive the account number where the funds are to be transferred. You will not know how this information will arrive. Please understand it *will* arrive. You must have the funds ready as you will have only five minutes to complete the transfer once you receive the information."

Richard ended the call.

"What do you think, Victoria? Are you worth two-million?"

"If he pays it, you'll go and leave us alone?" Victoria asked, searching his blank face.

A burst of wind buffeted the trailer. Pieces of debris pecked at the siding. Victoria looked up at the window but didn't move from her chair.

He saw her glance up at the window. "A little storm isn't going to change our plans. When I'm in the trailer I'll let you out of this room. However, you'll wear two pairs of cuffs—one for your ankles and one for your wrists. When I'm getting supplies you'll be locked in the bedroom without the cuffs. I've reinforced the bedroom and the bathroom—windows are nailed shut and covered with chicken wire so don't get any ideas of trying to break out. I'm leaving for awhile so be a good girl and eat your bagel. I'm not sure when I'll be back. There's water and a couple of sandwiches in the box I put on the bed."

He stood up, pushed the chair back out of the bedroom, and clamped the padlock shut behind him. Victoria tiptoed to the door trying to hear if he had left. Instead she heard him talking on the phone to someone he called Billy.

———

RICHARD PICKED UP HIS windbreaker, hesitated—his hand on the doorknob to leave. He saw the tube containing two of his paintings. With his heart pounding against the walls of his chest, he carefully took the cap off the end of the tube and gently pulled out his last two watercolors. He had painted the portraits in his condo—one after his first meeting with Victoria in the bookstore. She was smiling out at him, the silk scarf draped softly around her neck. In the second she was lying on the bed after he made love to her. Her violet eyes soft, full of love, begging him to come to her, to make love to her again. His eyes lingered over her image. Jerking his head up he quickly rolled the paintings together, stuffing them back in the tube. Throwing the tube on the counter he turned and left the trailer.

Glancing at the clouds building in the west, he hurried down to the end of the dock and threw the cell phone he had used to call Babcock into the water. Retracing his steps, he climbed into his car and backed away on the dirt path.

Chapter 29

July 13, Tuesday, 10:32 A.M.

THE LACE CURTAIN IN Mildred's front window moved a crack as one car after another parked in front of the Brookfield house. First in line was a big man in a white sedan. Marshal Ken Fisher introduced himself to Harri and told him he was now in charge of his case. His former handler had been reassigned to San Diego. Harri had called the marshal the night before and again this morning after receiving the ransom demand.

Next came a man driving a black SUV followed by a woman in a small, gray sedan. Both had visited Brookfield the evening before. The visitors disappeared through the front door. None rang the bell—the door opened immediately and quickly closed behind each arrival.

Kelly had brewed a large pot of coffee and Harri invited each new visitor to pick up a cup of coffee if they so desired. All accepted and then took a seat around the kitchen table. Fisher was not happy that Harri had called the Daytona Beach Police Department, Captain Salinas, and a private investigator, Miss Stitchway. However, because both of them arrived within minutes after he did, Fisher decided to let them stay—for the time being. Introductions were made accompanied by brief handshakes. Kelly stood at the kitchen window leaning back against the counter, her feet constantly shifting as she crossed and uncrossed her arms over her chest. Fisher immediately took control of what had become a conference.

"Harrison, tell me exactly what the caller said." Fisher, a young man in his early thirties, was an imposing figure of over two-hundred pounds—no fat. He was dressed in a suit and tie, and a stern face.

"The call was short. Said he had my wife." Harri stood up and started pacing. He stopped in front of Kelly patting her arm. "He wants me to wire two million dollars—that's how he said it, two million in two days. I will somehow receive the account number. Then he hung up."

"Did you recognize the voice?" Manny asked.

Harri looked at Manny but saw through him. Thinking. "No."

"What would you guess his age—young, old, a smoker, anything unusual about his voice?" Liz asked.

Harri sat back down. "Age … I don't know. Not real old. I would say he wasn't a smoker. His voice was clear. I'm sorry, nothing unique."

Fisher tapped the worn, white legal pad on the table in front of him with his pen. "Okay, tell me what happened last night. When did you first think your wife was missing?"

"Kelly, tell the marshal about the mall."

Kelly pulled a stool out from under the end of the counter, perched up on it, resting her feet on the rungs, hands clasped together in her lap. She related the same story she had told Manny and Liz the night before.

"So, there still hasn't been any communication with your mother?" Fisher asked, finishing his notes.

"That's right," Kelly replied, wrapping her arms around her body.

"Have you tried her cell again?" Fisher asked.

"Yes, but it goes to voicemail," Harri said. "No answer."

"Last night and this morning, Liz and I checked her email and her FaceBook account. She was—" Kelly looked at her father. "I'm sorry, Dad," she whispered.

"It's okay. Tell the marshal."

"It seems she's been seeing someone, a man. His name is Richard. The messages were pretty intimate."

"Which could mean she went voluntarily," Fisher said.

"But the ransom call—" Manny started to say.

"It could still be voluntary and they both want to shake you down, Harrison," Fisher said.

"Do you have that kind of money, Mr. Brookfield?" Liz asked.

"Yes. I started another company a few years after Vicky and I entered the WITSEC program. I—"

"Dad?" Kelly said.

"Witness Security program. I had developed and patented cyber protection software for the PC and Apple computer as well as a new chip design--faster. Another company bought me out but as part of the deal I receive significant royalties and they retain me as a consultant. I continued to enhance the program and am designing other programs and refining the chip in their research and development division."

"Why do you live so modestly, if you have that kind of money?" Liz asked, helping herself to another cup of coffee.

"You obviously don't understand how WITSEC works, Miss Stitchway. Witnesses are to maintain a *very* low profile," Fisher said without looking up from his notepad.

Liz raised her brows at Manny but did not offer a retort.

"In the beginning, when we first entered WITSEC," Harri continued, "we feared I would be found. We thought the man who killed my partner would surely be found and arrested. We never really felt safe."

"Maybe that's part of the answer. It's more than the money. Victoria couldn't take it anymore and found someone who would remove her from the situation," Fisher said, absent mindedly clicking the top of his pen several times. "A situation she didn't create."

"NO!" Kelly blurted out. "She wanted to hear about my interview. I'm sure she didn't run away."

Harri went to his daughter, folded her in his arms. Kelly nudged him back. No longer a little girl, she didn't cry. She was ready to help find her mother.

Looking over at Harri, who now appeared to see his daughter in a different light—grown up overnight, Fisher said, "I checked your case file, Harrison. The man you saw kill your partner remains wanted for murder. Unfortunately, we still don't know who he is— no name, only the description you gave at the time. He's never been located."

Fisher poured himself another cup of coffee. Sitting back down, he looked at Liz and then at Manny. "Harrison should not have involved you. However, we don't know yet if Victoria's disappearance has anything to do with the murder eleven years ago, or whether we have a lonely wife who has run away with her new lover … and … she thinks *they* can extort money to live happily ever after. So, let's work together. For now. Captain Salinas, you concentrate on the angle of a shake down. I'll see what else I can dig up in the case records—try to find a connection somewhere. We do know they have Harrison's original name—Herbert Babcock. Miss Stitchway, I'm not sure where that leaves you."

Both Harri and Manny spoke up at the same time. "She's working for me."

Liz looked from one to the other. Fisher cocked his head. "Well, Miss Stitchway, good luck. You seem to be blessed with two bosses. I'm going to put a tap on your phone, Harrison. We can patch it through to your office, Captain, as well as mine. You and Kelly will be recorded every time you receive a call or make a call. Harrison, do you have a cell?"

"Yes." He looked at Kelly.

"And Kelly, of course, does," Fisher said. "Let us know immediately if you receive a call from Victoria or the ransom man on either of your cell phones. I'd like you to refrain from answering your cells so he's forced to leave a message or call your home phone. Give us a chance to put on a trace. In which case, Captain, you are responsible for tracing. Kelly and Harrison, after a call to your cell phones are disconnected, if you want to call the person back, go ahead. For the time being I ask you both to keep your cell usage to a minimum."

Fisher wrote a few words on his pad and turned to a clean page.

"Now, we have two, make that three more considerations," Fisher said once again thumbing the end of his pen. "When the time comes to pay the ransom, we have to be ready to stall, keep him from realizing there will be no payment. That—"

"Oh, no," Harri said, standing up, leaning on the table as he stared at Fisher. "The money is ready. I transferred the funds to my bank account immediately after I called you. This is my wife we're talking about."

"Harrison, calm down. I can't stop you from making the payment, but I sure can tell you why you shouldn't. We'll discuss it later." Harri left the kitchen, muttering under his breath. No one spoke. The only sound was Fisher again thumbing the end of his pen—clicking in, out.

Harri came back, looked at Kelly, and sat down. "What are the *other* considerations," he asked steadying his coffee cup in both hands as he took a sip.

"That the killer has surfaced and then this account thing—the ransom. *If* Victoria was kidnapped, then it's more than likely the killer has her and figures he can get some money before he kills you. We have to put your house under surveillance for at least the next forty to seventy-two hours. Captain, can your cruisers swing by here on a random schedule?"

"Sure ... but what about you Feds picking up some of the tab?"

Fisher looked at Manny, then back at his pen. It appeared he had no intention of answering.

"Keep in mind," Fisher said, "that the killer's ultimate plan is to keep you, Harrison, from testifying. To be successful, he must kill you."

Chapter 30

HEARING RICHARD'S CAR PULL away from the trailer, Victoria began searching the room for a means of escape. But it seemed he had thought of every possibility. The only door was bolted from the other side. While a strong man might have broken through it, she did not possess that strength. She peered, pushed, pounded every which way on the bedroom and bathroom windows. As he said, they were nailed shut and reinforced with wire. The carpeting was glued down. If there was a loose floorboard she couldn't find it.

Opening the box he put on the bed, she snatched up one of the bottles of water, unscrewed the cap and sat cross-legged in the middle of the bed taking a long drink. Her eyes darted around the room as she drank and came to rest on the closet. Screwing the cap back on the water bottle, she scrambled off the bed and opened the closet door. Her purse was on the floor where he had thrown it after carrying her comatose body into the bedroom the evening before. Grabbing it, she dumped the contents out on the bed, snatched her cell and held it to her heart. "Thank, God," she whispered, her eyes closed tight. "He didn't find my phone."

She took three quick steps to the only window in the room. Pointing the phone to get the maximum image she could of the trees with the water beyond, she took a picture then quickly closed the phone to save the battery life. There was no way to get a photo of the outside of the trailer—size, color, or any description. But when Richard opened the door with her coffee earlier she saw a galley kitchen and a small living room beyond. From the dark paneling on the walls and the musty odor, she surmised the trailer was old, or hadn't been occupied for a long time, or maybe used only for camping. The dark green carpeting was very thin, like indoor-outdoor carpet, but soft.

She checked the bathroom for any clues as to the make or model of the trailer, or any other distinguishing features. There were none that she could see.

Back in the bedroom she returned all the items to her purse and began composing in her head what she would say in the text message to Harri. She didn't want to call him for fear the phone would die before she told him everything. Again, texting might save the battery so she could send additional messages. Finally ready with the words, she opened her phone. Knowing her husband rarely used his cell, she decided to send the text to Kelly.

> "Kelly, I've been kidnapped. Don't know where I am. Sending pic from trailer window. I'm OK. Not sure about another text. Battery low. Check my email for man: name Richard Stiles. Says he'll kill Harri if I run. LU mom."

She sent the message, then the picture. A warning blinked at her from the phone's display: "Battery Low"

She hid the phone in the bottom of her purse covering it with the other items, returned the purse to the floor of the closet, and pulled the accordion door shut.

Heaving a deep sigh, she had done all she could do at the moment. What she needed was a shower and a change of clothes. There was a dresser against the wall opposite the closet. Finding only men's clothes, she pulled out a pair of jeans, a white undershirt, and a pair of socks. All were a medium size. The belt she had worn with her capris would hold up the jeans. Taking a quick, freezing-cold shower in the tiny stall, she redressed in the clothes she found and then laid down on the bed to wait for Richard to return.

Suddenly she sat up, looked around, then jumped off the bed and ran to the closet. She thought she remembered seeing something in the back, but what was it? Pushing the door open, she got down on her hands and knees and inched forward. With the dappled light coming through the chicken wire on the window, she could see a case leaning against the far wall. She reached out, pulled it to her, and backed out of the closet.

Sitting on the floor, she ran her fingers over the soft, black leather.

"I've seen this before. If I'm not mistaken, it's the case Richard had when we met at the bookstore. His present … the scarf was in it and a sketchpad," she said softly.

Victoria climbed back on the bed. Sitting Indian style, she carefully unzipped the case. The pad was gone but in its place were pages of drawings almost the thickness of a ream of paper. She wasn't sure what she was looking at, but then it became clear, very obvious these were pen and pencil drawings of men in prison. There was nothing pretty about them. Loneliness, despair, anger, fear— emotions portrayed jumped off the paper at her.

Reaching for the bottle of water, she slowly drank, her eyes glued to the drawings. One by one she leafed through them, then stopped. She was looking at a drawing of Richard, a self portrait. His eyes were steely revealing deep hatred. He had long black hair and a beard, but she knew it was Richard—he was a prisoner.

Victoria set the portrait aside and continued to leaf through the pages. Again she stopped, her hand poised in the air, holding a drawing of the most grotesque man she had ever seen. Shuddering, she looked closer. The man had a pudgy face but there was nothing sweet about him. A deep scar ran from his right ear to his jaw. He looked sinister. No, worse. He looked evil. She put it to the side under Richard's self-portrait. Carefully, she continued leafing through the remaining drawings. There were no other drawings of himself or the evil-looking man.

Stacking the drawings together, she returned them to the case placing the two she had set aside on top of the others. She zipped the case shut and returned it to the closet, laying it next to her purse. She pulled the closet door shut and returned to the bed. Unwrapping one of the sandwiches, smiling at the peanut butter and jelly inside, she tried to grasp the meaning of what she had seen.

"He's been in prison," she whispered. "That's obvious because there's no way he could have captured the emotion in those prisoner's eyes, the way they held their bodies, if he hadn't witnessed it firsthand. Oh, the hatred in his own eyes." She shuddered again remembering the look on his face. She opened her mouth to take another bite of her sandwich but the drawing of the evil man flipped into her mind, and she put the remainder of the sandwich back in the box.

"Maybe Richard killed Harri's partner. No ... can't be or Harri would have testified and we'd be out of the protection program long before now. Wait a minute. The evil looking man was not in prison garb like all the others. It's clear Richard hates him from how he's portrayed." She leaned back against the headboard and sighed. "It's also clear that Richard is a very talented artist."

Victoria took another sip of water, closed her eyes, and felt Richard's warm lips on hers. Her eyes snapped open.

"Stop it, Victoria. For God's sake, he could walk in here and ... and ... kill you. No, he won't. He said he wouldn't hurt me. There's a man somewhere inside him that loves me. I know it. But which Richard will come back here. The one who will let me go, or the one who will continue to hold me for ransom and ...and kill me?"

A bolt of lightning struck in the distance followed by a sharp crack and rolling thunder.

Chapter 31

THE DBPD CONFERENCE ROOM was small and stuffy, but Elizabeth Stitchway, hunched over the large oak table, didn't notice the stale, humid air. With a clicker in her hand, she was scrutinizing the videos the mall security office had sent to Manny. The CD labeling system left much to be desired and, of course, she didn't know which exit the kidnapper took.

There was one main entrance into the mall but each major department store had several large entrances—Macy's, JC Penney, Sears, Dillard's, and a few others. A map of the mall lay on the table in front of Liz. The corner deli was circled where Kelly thought her mom was going to buy coffee, plus the bistro table Kelly sat at texting her friend Carol. Three different pictures of Vicky laid side-by-side next to the map.

This is like trying to find a grain of pepper in an anthill, Liz thought. She knew she wouldn't be lucky enough to find a shot of Vicky's face on the surveillance video, so all she had to go on was Vicky's shoulder-length black hair, brown T-shirt, and white capris. Of course, the CD's where black and white—so much for the T-shirt.

A CD labeled Macy's gave Liz her first sighting. The date and time stamp in the lower corner of the video was July 12, 4:16 p.m. Two cameras mounted above Macy's large display windows on the front of the store covered the expanse of trees, tables, and benches leading into the store.

Liz clicked the control freezing the frame. Kelly was sitting at the table looking down and just moving away was the back of a woman—dark T-shirt and white capris. "Finally," Liz whispered letting out a sigh. "Now, Vicky, lead me to your captor."

Liz clicked the control again to continue the video and followed the white Capris to the deli and coffee shop. The woman walked to the end of the line, stopped, looked up to her left, and walked quickly around the corner out of view.

"No, no. Vicky, where did you go?" The surveillance video ended.

Liz looked at the map and drew a line from the location where Kelly was sitting to the coffee shop and then around the corner. *The kidnapper is a pro,* she thought. *He knew he'd be caught on camera so he called to her. She knew him or she wouldn't have walked so fast to meet him.*

"Now, if I can figure out which CD is outside on the west end of the mall. JC Penney is the only store on the west end—no entrance on the west but there are entrances on the south and north side."

Liz flipped through the CDs and found three labeled JCP. The first one was inside the store. The second one was outside, south entrance. With time definitely around 4:15 to maybe 4:45, Liz jumped the video to 4:15 and let it run. Nothing. Picking up the third CD, north entrance she jumped the video again to 4:15.

"Whoa. There you are Vicky." Liz froze the frame, jumped up and did a fist pump just as Manny came through the door with two coffee mugs.

"Hey, watch out, Stitch." Both mugs were full. Hot coffee sloshed over the edge as Manny veered to miss Liz jumping around.

"I found her. I found her. Oh, sorry." Liz took a mug waving her fingers in the air flinging off the drips of coffee from the bottom. "I really need this. Thanks." She took a big swallow and gagged. "Ick. What? You added a whole stock of sugar cane?"

"I did not. I'm sorry it's not to your liking—one packet of Sweet and Low is all. I forgot you don't take sugar but I'll certainly remember next time," Manny said hitting the edge of the table with his mug spilling more coffee.

"Don't get huffy. Just a little cream next time. But thanks for the thought." She set her mug on the table, pushed it out of the way, then mopped up Manny's mess with a paper napkin.

"Here, let me show you something," Liz said, tossing the dripping napkin in the wastebasket.

She enlarged the frame showing the back of a woman walking in white capris, then freezing the video on a white SUV with a woman sitting in the back seat with a man.

"Can you get that big enough so we can see the license plate?" Manny asked.

Liz enlarged the frame again. "It's a California plate." She wrote the tag's numbers on her notepad, tore off the sheet and handed it to Manny, making a note of the number for herself on the next sheet.

Advancing the video, they saw the man slide out of the backseat but the woman was no longer visible. He shut the door, hurried to the driver's side, got in and slowly drove off out of camera range.

Liz stopped the video and looked at Manny. "He drugged her or knocked her out with something. She had to be lying on the back seat."

Manny pushed his chair back and began pacing around the small room, shoving chairs out of his way. "Stitch, we're running out of time."

Chapter 32

―――

July 13, Tuesday, 4:00 P.M.

POLLY SAT AT A LITTLE square table for two by the window in McDonalds. She was waiting for Anthony, another date, thanks to SeniorFriendFinder's website. She would have preferred Panera Bread, but, what the heck, coffee is coffee.

It was four o'clock—Anthony said it was a good time for him. A group of three high-school kids wandered in, ordered a #2 special, and then sat at a large table in the back laughing and talking as they opened their meals. A woman, then two men bustled in and ordered coffee. One added an apple pie.

A van drove up with a sign—Lake View Manor—on the side and stopped at the curb. A man stepped tentatively down the van's two steps with the aid of the driver's steady hand. The man waited as the driver lifted a walker placing it on the sidewalk. The two said a few words and the man turned and strolled, with the aid of his walker, into McDonalds. It wasn't until then that Polly saw his face.

"Oh my, that's Anthony." *Now what do I do? You behave like the polite lady you are Polly Pringle.*

The man navigated the door, hesitated, looked around, and then a smile crossed his face when he spotted Polly. He whirled right over to her, the wheels in front of the walker turning smartly followed by the back legs encased in bright-yellow tennis balls.

Polly instantly stood up and pulled the chair opposite from where she was sitting away from the table so the man could sit down.

He had other thoughts, however, and shot his hand out to her. "You look just like your picture, Polly, only prettier. I'm Anthony."

"It's nice to meet you, Anthony ... in person. I thought I'd get a cup of coffee. What can I bring you?"

"I'd like one of those strawberry milkshakes, (delete "," after "milkshakes") if you please," he replied. "Wait, wait a minute, I have the money. I'm a bit old fashioned—the man pays for the drinks," he said a twinkle in his eyes as he pulled a worn, brown-leather wallet from his pants pocket, handing Polly a ten-dollar bill.

"Well, thank you, Anthony. I'll be right back."

Polly returned with their drinks but instead of coffee she opted for a strawberry milkshake along with Anthony. They chitchatted as other patrons came and went.

Anthony told her that at three different times he had flat-lined during an operation, but he had fooled them. He liked the assisted-living home where he stayed for the past two years but longed to see a pretty woman such as Polly. It was at this point he asked her if she played cards.

"As a matter of fact, I enjoy a hot game of gin now and then," she replied with a wink.

"Do you think you could come over and play sometime?" he asked.

"I think I might be able to do that," she said taking a final pull on her straw sucking nothing but fizz, she laughed. "Sorry. Please excuse me. It's been awhile since I've had a milkshake."

In reply, Anthony sucked on his straw making the same sound. They both grinned and laughed at their faux pas.

Suddenly the date was over. His driver walked over to let him know he had returned to pick him up. Anthony stood taking hold of his walker the driver had positioned in front of him.

"Thank you, Polly. I enjoyed meeting you immensely. I'll send you an invitation to play cards."

"I enjoyed our date too, Anthony. Thanks for the milkshake."

Polly overheard him tell the driver as they exited the restaurant, "Just wait till the boys see Polly when she visits to play cards with me."

———

AFTER A FEW ERRANDS Polly was back home sitting at her computer, writing to tell Sam about her date.

Sam immediately replied:

> HotMail, July 13, 5:10 pm
>
> "Flat-lined three times did he. I'm surprised after seeing you he just didn't up and die figuring he was in heaven. However, I have a good one to tell you about my date last night for drinks—I know, I know, only coffee on a first date but I was thirsty and her picture looked pretty good.
>
> Anyway, I'm drinking my Manhattan and I begin to notice things. Like, besides the deep voice, her hands were not dainty, but actually rather large. Then her face—a squarish jaw. She crossed her legs and one foot was protruding out from under the table—it was quite big even though she had on a pair of heels.
>
> Well, I looked at Charlene, right in the eyes, and I said, yes, I did, I said, are you a man? You know what she said? She said, 'Yes I am, but I like playing a woman and you said you were looking for companionship and I thought, what the hell, I can do companionship.'
>
> Polly, I'm still laughing. We had another drink and then I excused myself. I didn't say I'd see her, or him, again. Your friend, Sam."

Polly wiped the tears from her eyes from laughing. She was about to reply to Sam when she heard a ping. Sam had sent her another message.

> HotMail, July 13, 5:16 pm
>
> "Polly, why haven't we met each other. I've enjoyed your messages very much. How about coffee tomorrow at four, if that's good for you? I like Panera Bread but am certainly open to your suggestion. What do you say? Sam.

PS: If you're a man please don't reply. I couldn't take it again. Ha Ha."

Polly attacked the keyboard.

"Not a man? I guess I'll just have to leave my cigars at home. See you tomorrow. Your friend, Polly."

Chapter 33

LIZ WIPED THE BEADS of perspiration off her forehead with a hand towel, keeping her eyes on the road except for a quick glance now and then at the darkening clouds hovering overhead. She turned on her car radio for the latest information on the storm front as she turned into the Brookfield driveway. The weather lady reported that the storm was about to be upgraded from a Category 1 to a Category 2 Hurricane. Sustained winds were blowing above seventy-four miles per hour. The track had shifted slightly and was now expected to graze the west coast of Florida.

Harri was waiting at the front door. She hurried to join him and they went straight to the kitchen.

"Hi, Liz," Kelly said. "I'm getting to be a pro at this coffee thing. Want a cup?"

"Please and a spot of cream if you have it. Harri, I found your wife on the mall's security surveillance video. She got into a white SUV with a man—couldn't see his face, or hers for that matter. But from what Kelly said she was wearing, and the date and time stamp on the video, I'm sure I have the right woman. Thanks, Kelly." Liz paused to take a sip of coffee savoring the sugar-free taste and then filled the two of them in on the details of the sighting.

Kelly heard her cell and jumped to pull it out of her jeans. "Dad, it's mom's ringtone." Checking her phone, she squealed, "She sent me a text. She says she's been kidnapped. And ... there's a picture."

Harri grabbed the phone from Kelly's outstretched hand. "She says she's not hurt. I can't make out much from this picture. It's out a window, grainy, through a screen. Liz, take a look." He put the phone into Liz's outstretched hand.

"She's showing us where she is ... near water. Kelly, is this from her cell phone, her cell code?"

"Yes." Kelly gasped for breath.

"Okay, if I take your phone?" Liz called out over her shoulder as she raced out of the kitchen to the front door. I have to get this to Manny—maybe he can ping her location."

Kelly and Harri ran after Liz but her car was already rolling out of the driveway, turned and sped down the street.

The curtain on Mildred's front window fell back into place.

Chapter 34

July 13, Tuesday, 6:20 P.M.

MANNY PACED AROUND HIS office, Peaches on his heels. He gave her a pat on the head and then sat tapping his calendar desk pad with his pen. One of his detectives, Fred Watson, had called in about an abandoned white SUV and Manny was waiting to hear if it was the vehicle involved in the Brookfield kidnapping.

"Peaches, how long can it take Fred to verify that the car has a California plate … or not?" He began pacing again. His phone rang and Manny lunged for it.

It was the desk sergeant. "Just to let you know, Captain, an officer brought in a DUI, a young woman, a very belligerent woman, and we may need—"

"Sergeant, tell the officer to book her." Manny slammed the phone down. It instantly rang again. "Sergeant, I can't—"

"Excuse me, Captain. A black and white just reported an abandoned car. Your detective found an SUV left overnight in back of Wal-Mart. He called in the Vehicle Identification Number. It was purchased four months ago in San Francisco."

"Stop! Patch me through to the officer." *Maybe we're getting a break.*

"Detective Watson."

"Fred, that car you found, any chance of tracking down the owner?" Manny clipped, his voice rising in exasperation.

"The VIN traced to a dealer in California. I talked to him and he said the man who bought the car paid cash. I checked the name on the bill of sale—it was a phony."

"Anything else?"

"No plate. But the description matches the APB you put out last night and it was a California plate you saw on the surveillance video. It was wiped clean—very professional."

"Have someone from the garage pick it up."

"Manny."

"Yes!"

"I did a preliminary search. As I said it was clean but I did find a couple strands of hair—black, about eight inches long caught in the fabric of the back seat. I'm on my way to the lab."

"Stop at the Brookfield's and get a comb, hairbrush, anything with Mrs. Brookfield's DNA."

———

LIZ JUMPED OUT OF her car, dashed through the DBPD entrance and asked the desk sergeant to tell Captain Salinas that Elizabeth Stitchway was at the desk.

"Tell him I have to see him. Tell him to hurry," Liz commanded.

The sergeant looked at Liz—didn't make a move. Liz could see the sergeant thought she was a crazy woman. The sergeant slowly turned to her console and put a call through to the captain, mumbled something and hung up. Liz marched back and forth from the entrance to the bank of elevators. The elevator dinged and the door slid open.

"Stitch, what the heck are you doing here, I thought we were—"

"Kelly … I just left Brookfield's … here … the phone." Liz raised her hand with Kelly's phone just missing Manny's nose.

"Take a breath. What's with the phone?"

Liz took a deep breath. "Oh, I don't know. Kelly received a text from Mrs. Brookfield—"

Manny grabbed the phone from Liz's hand and hustled to the elevator.

"Stay here," he called over his shoulder. "We'll try to ping the tower. Get her location."

The elevator door slid shut.

Chapter 35

IT WAS DUSK WHEN Razor parked in the shadows next to a black sedan at the Down-the-Hatch restaurant. He was anxious to wrap up this meeting and get back to the trailer and Victoria, but Pit Bull insisted on seeing him now. Bull had landed at the Daytona Beach Airport two hours earlier. Bull arranged the meeting with Razor by cell phone, giving him time to rent a car, register at a motel, and rendezvous with Razor.

Razor, his stomach clenched in a knot, struggled with himself—should he trigger his plan or wait. It all depended on how Bull treated him. He locked the car at the same time Bull climbed out of his rental, grumbling that in the future he'd ask for a bigger car. The two men performed the obligatory brief hug and then ambled to the restaurant's deck, staying in the shadows. Slipping into the end of the outdoor bar, each ordered a whiskey with a beer chaser. Returning quickly with their drinks, the waiter asked if they wanted to order an appetizer. The kid shifted from one foot to the other. He kept glancing to the west at the advancing clouds. Bull was hungry and settled on the Fisherman's Platter. Razor asked for a grilled fish sandwich. They told the waiter they were moving to a high-top table out of the breeze.

Neither man spoke. Both sipped their drinks as they gazed at the Halifax River. The water was usually blue—reflecting the sky. Now, there were no streaks of gold from the western sun. The water was black and murky.

The young waiter hustled to the table balancing their orders. He placed the dishes on the high top and turned to leave.

"Hey, you," Bull called to the waiter. "Bring me and my friend here another shot."

Bull dug into a piece of deep-fried white fish, wiped his mouth and took another bite. "Will you have my money tomorrow?" he asked, chewing as he gazed at the river.

"Not tomorrow. It'll be a couple of days before Babcock can get it together."

"Bull shit. He's stalling or you're stalling. You've been here over a month. Maybe I should give the job to somebody else. Let him split the money."

"Yea? Like who else could pull this off?"

"Like maybe that punk that walked out of prison with you. All I'm saying is I want the money in my account now. The bastard owes me, and then you bring him to me so I can see the shock on his face when he sees me after all these years." Bull chuckled. "Who knows, maybe he forgot what I look like. I should have hung around after I threw that package at you."

"Well thanks a lot. You put me away in the slammer. And they almost pinned that murder on me. You owe me big time." *Wait a minute. What did he just say—'maybe he forgot what I look like?' Did he shoot the guy?*

"I paid you good. You should be grateful—more money than most earn in that amount of time—tax free."

Razor felt the heat rising under his collar but he didn't tip his hand. He had, however, made up his mind to start to settle the score. His revenge for those wasted years in prison. "What did you mean by bring him to you?"

"Now, Razor, you think Babcock is gonna walk up to me, shake hands, and say it's nice to see you again? He's the only one that can testify my connection to the drugs. I'm gonna silence him once and for all."

Oh, the drugs, sure, maybe it was just the drugs. "You'll surprise him all right," Razor said downing the last drop of whiskey. "Order me another shot. I'm going to hit the can."

Razor walked back in the shadows toward the restroom but swerved out to the parking lot. He quickly opened the trunk of his car, retrieving a pint-size, zip-lock bag wrapped in brown paper and closed the lid. He opened the driver's side of Bull's car, stuffing the package under his seat, and shut the door. *Didn't even lock his car— Bull's getting careless in his old age. He made it easy for me— payback time.* Razor ambled back to the bar by way of the men's room. He picked up his shot glass and threw the amber liquid down his throat in one gulp.

"I have to get going. See how Mrs. Babcock is doing."

"You aren't messing around with her are ya?"

"Only enough to whisk her away in the car without screaming. Always protecting your interests, Bull. I'll be in touch tomorrow."

Razor slid off the bar stool, leaving the tab for Bull to pay. He heard Bull order another shot as he melted into the shadows.

Chapter 36

—

July 13, Tuesday, 9:00 P.M.

VICTORIA HEARD THE LOW hum of a car rolling to a stop. Sitting up in bed she switched on the corroded brass lamp on the bedside table and waited to see which Richard was returning to the trailer.

She didn't have long to wait. She heard him bolt the front door, throw his keys down, and his footsteps approaching her door. Unlocking the door, he pushed it open with his shoulder and stood a moment looking at her. His eyes were warm—his jaw slacked. Did he want to tell her something?

"Here's your dinner," he said, placing a white take-out container on the bed. "Sorry it's so late. My errands took longer than I expected. You can bring it out to the kitchen if you like."

He turned and walked out leaving the door open. She picked up the box and slowly walked out of the room, her eyes darting around the space she'd only glimpsed before.

Richard was sitting in a threadbare easy chair, his feet up on a rickety, wooden chair with scratched black paint. A glass of milk was on the small table beside him.

"Help yourself to milk, beer, or whatever you find in the fridge." He opened his white container and picked up a half-eaten sandwich.

A calm feeling flowed through Victoria's body. He was distant, but she didn't fear him. She hid the feelings she had earlier—after all, he had used her to get at Harri. Everything he said to her before was only part of a plot to obtain a big ransom. She poured a glass of milk and then sat on the musty brown sofa facing him. Opening the box with her dinner, she looked up at his face. He looked tired, very tired. He bit off a small piece of his sandwich, set it back down, and chewed with his eyes closed. He obviously trusted her not to try to escape.

Victoria steeled herself not to go to him, to tell him to sleep. He had opened a world to her that afternoon in his condo, and she would hold the memory of their time together in her heart. But he was a mystery, and she was Mrs. Harrison Brookfield—wife and mother, and she was going to return to that life, that person.

"Richard," she whispered.

He didn't move from the chair, his feet remained on the make-shift stool, but his eyes opened. She was startled to see the sadness they held. He said nothing—he didn't have to. His eyes told her everything as he looked at her.

"I found some drawings in the back of the closet," she said softly. "Drawings of prisoners. You were in prison ... for a long time." It was not a question. It was a statement. The only sign that he heard what she said was a raised eyebrow. She continued to stare at him. Waiting.

"Yes."

She barely heard the word. "There's a drawing of you—long hair, a beard. Is it a self-portrait?"

He nodded, yes, barely moving his head.

"Are the drawings ... all of them, yours?"

"Yes. All mine." He spoke quietly without emotion, never taking his eyes from hers.

"There was a drawing of a man, not a prisoner—he must have done something terrible to you."

"Yes. But, it doesn't matter. It'll all be over soon."

A gust of wind rocked the trailer. The lights flickered but remained on.

"It's late," Richard said. "You'd better go to bed. You haven't eaten your sandwich. Do you want to take it in your room?"

"Yes. Thank you." Victoria picked up the glass of milk, holding the white box in her other hand. She took a couple of steps toward the bedroom, stopped, turning to face him. His eyes remained on her.

"Why were you in prison?"

"Dealing drugs. I was framed. They thought I was the leader of a gang. I was in the next room when your husband's partner was killed.

"But—"

"The Feds tried to pin the murder on me, but your husband didn't identify me as the killer in the lineup."

"Because you weren't the man he saw."

"Good night, Victoria."

She walked into the bedroom. Dismissed. Richard bolted the door behind her.

Chapter 37

———

July 13, Tuesday, 10:00 P.M.

BULL HAD A BAD feeling about his meeting with Razor. He'd run up against weasels before and Razor gave off all the vibes of a weasel tonight. If Babcock was stalling, maybe he needed a little persuasion. Bull wanted his money. Babcock owed him for all the funds he'd sunk into his business in San Francisco, and then the bastard blew the whistle and squashed a ten-million-dollar deal.

Well, I'd better line up some insurance, he thought, picking up his cell.

"Billy!"

"That you, Bull?"

"Yes, Billy, it's me." *Why do I have to deal with this knucklehead?*

"Well, this is a nice surprise. I was just thinking about you."

"How's that?"

"The last time I talked to Razor I asked him about my money. I've been working my buns off in dirt doing my part watching the Brookfield's for you. He said I'd get my cut … in time. So, Bull, when am I gonna get my money?"

"Soon, Billy, and there may be a bonus if you do something for me."

"Name it."

"I think Brookfield needs to be persuaded to release the money he owes me. I want you to get over there now and send a message through his front window. Let him know we mean business. Can you do that for me, Billy?"

"Sure. I'll leave now."

"Don't take that red truck of yours. Borrow a neighbor's car—a drive-by shooting. Don't give anyone a chance to see the license plate on the car. Douse the lights as you approach. And, Billy—"

"What?"

"For God's sake, don't kill him or there won't be any money for any of us. Got that!"

"Okay, Bull. Anything else?"

"Yea, don't tell that punk living with you where you're going."

———

HARRI SAT AT HIS computer checking the bank account for the umpteenth time.

"Dad?"

"Yes, Kel, come on in."

"I'm going to my room—maybe to bed soon. Anything I can get for you?"

"No. You run along."

"Do you think mom will be home tomorrow?"

"I sure hope—"

A gunshot ripped through the house. The sound of breaking glass accompanied the blast. Kelly screamed as Harri knocked her to the floor covering her with his body. Following the discharge the house was silent. The only lights were in the kitchen and the study, where Harri and Kelly laid on the floor.

"Stay here," Harri said. "Don't stand up."

Harri crawled down the hallway, inched around the corner to the living room. Small shards of glass were lying on the floor. He felt hot, humid air on his skin coming through the splintered window. Slowly lifting his head, Harri peeked out. Nothing moved in the yard or the street. Crawling to the front door, he checked that it was locked. Crawling from the front door to the kitchen, he flipped off the light. Then he walked to the back door and the door to the garage. Both were locked. He called to Kelly to reach up and turn off the desk lamp and the computer.

"Let your eyes adjust, then come in the kitchen. I'm calling Fisher." Harri dialed the marshal on his cell.

"Hello, Babcock, what's up?"

"Someone just tried to kill me, that's what's up. Someone shoots through my front window and I have to ask, where's my protection? Shit. Can't you law guys do something?"

"Are you hurt?" Fisher asked.

"No."

"Kelly?"

"She's scared. Hell, we both are."

"Salinas is probably alerted to your call by now, but I'll get in touch with him to be sure. A cruiser will no doubt be at your house any minute."

"Yah, (replace "Yah" with "Yes") I see him. Kelly, go let the officer in—ask him to identify himself before you open the door and stand ... no, wait. I'll go."

"Babcock."

"What?"

"Don't pay the money tomorrow. Give us one more day," Fisher said.

Harri slammed the phone back on the wall and went to answer the knock on the front door.

"Who is it?"

"Detective Watson."

Harri opened the door just as the phone rang. He ran back to the kitchen.

"What do you want?" Harri yelled into the receiver.

"I want the money tomorrow."

Harri expected the caller to be Fisher or Salinas. When he heard the kidnapper's voice, his blood ran cold.

"Well, all my funds haven't transferred so you're just going to have to wait another day. Maybe they'll never be ready. I'm real pissed off at the bullet you put through my front window."

"Listen, Babcock, I'll give you one more day and then you'll get the instructions for the wire transfer, sometime Thursday. As I said before, you'll have fifteen minutes or you won't see your wife again." The call disconnected.

Harri stood staring at the phone as the detective switched on the kitchen light, his cell to his ear. "Manny, did you trace the call?"

The detective closed his cell and looked up at Harri and Kelly watching him.

"Well?" Harri said.

"No trace. The call wasn't long enough."

Chapter 38

July 14, Wednesday, 10:00 A.M.

POLLY HASTILY ASSEMBLED THE Quilt-of-Valor group at Liz's request. The PI hoped someone in the group had seen something, anything that might help lead to Mrs. Brookfield. Liz had already met everyone at Rocket's party—Susan, Mildred and Polly. She didn't meet Kelly until the night her mother went missing.

Billy was working around the side of the house fertilizing the plants when the quilters arrived. The skies were growing ominous with gusty south-east winds. Everyone, including Kelly, was sitting at the dining room table when Liz walked in. She helped herself to coffee and then sat in the empty chair at the table. She made a few remarks about the latest reports on the impending storm then eased the conversation into Mrs. Brookfield's disappearance.

"Nothing, I have to tell," Susan Armstrong snipped. "Polly insisted I come to meet with you, but I'm only in this neighborhood when we meet to sew on the quilt."

Liz jotted a few words on her yellow pad. "Polly, anything come to your mind as you think back, not just since Mrs. Brookfield disappeared but prior to that … days … weeks?"

"Honestly, Liz—" Polly started to say.

"Well, something happened last night. I heard a gunshot. Scared me to death. Kelly, I saw a police car at your house," Mildred said, her hands folded on her yellow apron.

Kelly sighed. "It was a gunshot you heard. The police came out to investigate but … that was it."

Manny had emailed Liz about the incident. It seemed both the bad guys and good guys were getting frustrated with the lack of progress. Each with their own agenda.

"That gardener of yours," Mildred snapped.

"Billy?" Polly shot back, looking at Mildred.

"Yes, Billy. I've seen him watching Vicky. If she so much as steps a toe outside the house, he crosses my lawn and starts talking to her."

"Well, maybe once," Polly said, her voice pensive. "But, no—"

"Once, my foot," Mildred snapped again. "If he hadn't been at your house, Polly, the next morning, after you told me about Vicky, I'd say he did it or at least knows where she is. He's up to no good that man. I don't know why you hired him."

Liz watched the two women spar. "Why did you hire him, Polly," Liz asked keeping her tone of voice soft.

All eyes turned to Polly—nothing like a cat fight to speed-up the pulse rate between friends.

"Well, I ... I ... he stopped by the house—months ago—said he was working down the street and saw me wrestling with a bag of mulch in the trunk of my car."

"Were you? Trying to get mulch out of the trunk?" Susan asked, her tongue sharp.

"Yes, I was and the conversation led from one thing to another, and he asked if he could help me in the garden."

"How often does he come to help ... in your garden?" Liz asked.

"To begin with it was a couple times a month. But once May came and now summer, well, it's hard to keep up with it—the garden. I love my flowers and with Billy's help I've added several beds."

"What's Billy's last name?" Liz asked.

"I don't know. I always pay him in cash."

"Telephone number?"

"Yes. Let me get it for you."

———

11:12 A.M.

LIZ THANKED THE QUILTERS for meeting on such short notice. Susan darted out to her car and drove off. Kelly gave Liz a quick hug and said it was too bad her friends didn't have anything more to offer, but it was worth a try.

"Are you okay after the incident last night?" Liz asked.

"Not really. But what can I do ... you, the captain, and the marshal are working on it. I cleaned up the glass and dad put a patch on the window until he can get it replaced. A glass guy said he'd try to get to us today. We're bound to get some rain even if the hurricane doesn't come our way."

"Would you feel better if Captain Salinas asked an officer to stay with you?"

"No. Dad and I are coping. But maybe they should cruise by more often."

Liz walked down the sidewalk to her car, overhearing Polly chastise Mildred at the front door. Polly didn't appreciate what Mildred said about her gardener. Liz slid into her car, looked back, and saw Billy staring at her. She drove around the corner and turned into the parking lot for the Pelican Bay clubhouse.

Pulling her cell from her tote, she selected a number from her phone list.

"Manny, it's Liz."

"How did it go with the fearsome quilters?"

"Cut the sarcasm, Captain. It may be nothing but I suggest you pick up, or at least talk to Polly's gardener, Billy. No last name, but I have his telephone number."

Liz filled Manny in on the heated exchange between Polly and Mildred. She gave him the gardener's telephone number and told him that she had left Billy at Polly's house not more than three minutes ago. She thought Manny could find something wrong with the truck or better yet, say that he was talking to people in the neighborhood because Mrs. Brookfield's family was worried about her.

"Thanks, but I think I can handle him, Stitchway."

"Okay, okay. Did your detectives *handle* Kelly's cell?"

"Truce. Yes. The text bounced off a tower in Astor Park—almost an hour from here. It's in a field, west side of the St. John's River on Route 40." Two squad cars are out looking for a trailer.

"Manny, that's terrific."

"Well, yes and no. It's an old tower and the phone companies haven't upgraded their transmitters."

"That doesn't matter—the message made it to Kelly's cell."

"But Mrs. Brookfield's cell isn't on, or it's dead. We can't ping her phone from the tower. Kelly's cell has a GPS chip but her mother's doesn't. So either way—no chip, dead, or turned off—we're still looking at a wide radius. There's a patchwork of dirt roads—lots of campsites hidden in the pine and palm trees along the river. It's also rural so some people have trailers on their land."

"Any more on the shooting last night?"

"No, but Harri stalled the ransom payment until tomorrow at Fisher's request."

Chapter 39

———

MANNY BORROWED AN OFFICER'S gray coupe and drove to the Pelican Bay development. He parked behind a beat-up red truck in front of Polly Pringle's house. Dressed in all black street clothes, he sauntered up the walkway and rang her doorbell, nodding to the gardener. He noticed the lace curtain in the neighbor's front window move a tad.

Polly opened the door, and exclaimed, "Hello. Manny isn't it. My, this is a busy morning."

"Manny it is. I was in the neighborhood and thought I'd stop to say hello. How are you today?"

"Oh, fine, thank you. My friends and I met with that nice Elizabeth Stitchway this morning. In fact, you just missed them. Would you care for a cup of coffee—the girls didn't drink much," she said smiling.

"No, thanks anyway. I'm going to stop at a couple of your neighbors—you know, checking if they saw anything last night."

"Oh, that shooting. I heard the shot, but I honestly thought it was a motorcycle backfiring, so I didn't get up to investigate. I guess I should have."

"Yup. Keep your eyes and ears open, Polly. At least until Mrs. Brookfield comes home. Bye for now."

"Bye. Have a nice day."

Manny started walking across the lawn, saw the gardener and ambled over to him.

"Hi, those roses are certainly thriving. Mine always get eaten up by the bugs. You the gardener here?" Manny asked.

"Sure am," Billy answered.

"My name's Manny. You're?"

"Billy."

"Well, Billy, do you take on jobs for other people?"

"Sometimes. I'm pretty busy right now, but I have an assistant—he could use the work."

"He any good?"

"He's my apprentice—I tell him what to do."

"Mrs. Pringle only hires the best so, if you say your assistant can do the work, as long as you supervise, I'd like to talk to him. What's his name and how can I get a hold of him?"

"Lenny. He's staying with me for awhile so I'll have him call you," Billy said. He pulled a tag off one of the rose bushes and took a pencil from his pocket. "What's your number?"

Manny gave Billy his cell number, thanked him, and returned to his car. He gave a nod to Billy as he drove off.

———

12:05 P.M.

THE DAYTONA BEACH Police Department matched the telephone number Polly Pringle gave to Liz with the address at a mobile home park in the name of William Carter. The officer relayed the information to Manny and he immediately changed directions and drove to the park. While driving, he called Liz and told her where he was going—he'd call her later. He wasn't sure this Lenny person knew anything.

Pulling up in the short driveway of the mobile home, his eyes swept the surroundings through his dark glasses. Manny walked to the front door and knocked. A young man opened the door, a bottle of beer in his hand.

"Hi," Manny said. "I was just talking to Billy. Are you Lenny?"

"Yea. Why?"

"I met Billy at Mrs. Pringles. He said you're his assistant. Might like some work."

"I sure would. Come on in. Want a beer, Mr., Mr."

"Just call me Manny."

"Hell, Manny, I can do anything Billy can. Probably better and I sure need the work. I can't find anything around here."

"Not from Florida I take it," Manny said settling on the couch facing a worn overstuffed chair that Lenny had flopped in, his leg up over the arm waving his bare foot in the air.

"No. I'm a San Francisco boy. Me and a friend drove here a few weeks ago."

"That must have been quite a trip … you and your friend made. I like California—better than Florida—but what the heck. I bet you miss California."

"Yea, love it, but not the last year," Lenny said, swatting a fly off his big toe.

"Oh, why is that?" Manny asked leaning forward, elbows on his knees, scratching his ear.

"Me and my friend just got out of Folsom. Couple months ago. I was railroaded, Manny. Mistaken identity. Stupid cop said I held up this little store, a gas station with snacks and stuff … then, just cuz I had two other arrests, trumped up charges again, they hauled me off to Folsom for a year." Lenny shook his head in disbelief and then took a swig from his beer bottle.

"Oh, that's tough luck … that they railroaded you. Your friend find a job around here, or does he hang out with you and Billy?"

"Nah. He's got money, so he split. Told me to get a job. Keep my nose clean. Easy for him to say. You'd think he'd help me a little."

"Well, tell you what," Manny said. "I have a high school kid doing odd jobs for me this summer, but he's always goofing off with his pals. Let me talk to him and then I'll get back with you. I'm sure you'd be more reliable—needing money and all. You have a cell phone?"

"No, but you can use Billy's number. Let me write it down for you."

"Thanks, Lenny. By the way what's your last name?"

"Stewart. Leonard Stewart."

1:02 P.M.

"STITCH, MEET ME AT my office. No, make that the conference room. We have a connection to San Francisco. It could be significant. Don't know yet." Manny disconnected the call, stopped to fill his coffee cup from the dregs of the morning pot, touched his thigh inviting Peaches to come along, and then rode the elevator to the department's first-floor conference room, placing a call to Marshal Fisher on the way down.

"Manny. What's up?"

"We may have a break in the Brookfield case."

"Give it to me."

Manny filled the marshal in on Billy leading to Lenny, leading to Folsom Prison in California.

Liz hustled into the conference room and sat down across from Manny. Peaches stretched fore and aft then trotted eagerly to Liz. The happy dog, her tail thumping the side of the chair, was rewarded with a pat on her silky black head. Manny looked at Liz with a brief smile, put the phone on speaker, and then looked back to his notes.

"Lenny said he was released from Folsom Prison at the same time another prisoner was released," Manny said. "I didn't ask for his friend's name for fear I'd spook him. If this turns out to be relevant I'll pick him up. But right now I want to play it safe and let Billy, Lenny, and maybe the kidnapper, continue on the assumption we're not on to them."

"Sounds right. Lenny's last name?"

"Stewart. He was released after a one-year stint around two months ago. How long do you think it'll take you to get the name of his friend? This friend, according to Lenny, has money, and they drove from San Francisco to Daytona Beach together leaving immediately after they were released."

"I'll be back to you within the hour," Fisher said and hung up.

Manny and Liz locked eyes.

"I'm really worried about that shooting," Liz said. "Did your detective find the bullet or a casing?"

"The bullet was lodged in the living room wall opposite the window. Hit a stud. No casing yet. Let's run and get some take out," Manny suggested. "We can eat lunch here in the conference room while we wait for Fisher's call."

THE PAINTER | 157

"You stay here. I'll go. Where's Kelly's phone? I'll drop it off to her while I'm out."

"The desk Sergeant has it."

"What do you want for lunch—fillet mignon with tiny red potatoes and a side of asparagus?" Liz asked, slinging her tote over her shoulders.

"I was thinking more on the lines of a fish sandwich with fries," he said smiling "From Mickey D's."

"Good choice. Nothing like a batch of greasy fries when your stomach is on high alert working a kidnapping case."

———

1:52 P.M.

LIZ RETURNED WITH Manny's order and a duplicate for herself. He looked at her with raised brows.

"If you think I'm going to salivate over your fries, you're mistaken, mister police officer."

They dug into their sandwiches, both closing their eyes as they savored the rare treat of a batch of fries.

"Don't eat so fast," Liz quipped. "I'm not sharing. How's your—"

Manny's cell rang and was grabbed with greasy fingers. Seeing it was the marshal he hit the speaker button and laid the phone on the table wiping his fingers with a paper napkin Liz threw to him.

"Talk louder, Fisher. You're on speaker—Stitchway is with me."

"I said, I'm on I-4 heading your way. Traffic's snarled, lightning is picking up, but only sporadic rain. Fires are breaking out all over the place. Some roads are being closed."

"I don't need a weather report." Manny shook his head at Liz, opening his eyes wide. Liz shrugged her shoulders and popped the last fry in her mouth throwing a satisfied smile at Manny.

"Lenny Stewart was released the same day as a Robert Steele. Nickname: Razor. They walked out together."

"So why the rush to Daytona Beach?" Manny asked.

"Give me a chance, will you," Fisher said. "Steele was sent to Folsom on a drug possession charge—a bag on his body, but bricks of it in his car and in his apartment."

Manny let out a whistle, "That's a lotta crack."

"Wait, it gets better—watch out lady you almost hit me," Fisher yelled. "Where was I?"

"It gets better."

"Oh, yea. Razor was also charged with the murder of Babcock's partner but they couldn't make it stick. No evidence except he was in the building."

Manny and Liz shoved the apple pies back into the sacks, placed their notepads in front of them, and started writing.

"Hey, you guys still there? Manny?"

"Yep, we're here," Manny muttered. "Lenny said his friend didn't stay with Billy. He said he bought a condo or something. How far away from Daytona Beach are you?"

"Should be there in forty minutes—normally—but this traffic is awful."

"I'm going to have a couple of my officers bring Lenny and Billy in, separate them, see what we can turn up on who this Robert Steele may be. I don't want them to bolt or worse yet, alert Steele in case he's the one who has Mrs. Brookfield and sent the ransom demand."

Liz wrote some initials in big letters in the middle of a blank page on her notepad and turned it so Manny could see: RS = RS. Robert Steele = Richard Stiles???

Chapter 40

——

July 14, Wednesday, 2:00 P.M.

THE STORM SHIFTED AGAIN. The latest NOAA weather alert indicated that the hurricane had slowed over the Gulf, was growing in intensity, and could hit the western coast of Florida and potentially central Florida.

Sam and Polly exchanged several emails during the morning questioning if they should postpone the meeting due to the storm, but in the end they both wanted to go ahead with their date. With Sam's question of why they hadn't met, they were both eagerly looking to make it happen. Postponing was out of the question unless the storm was imminent. However, they did move the time up from four to two o'clock. This would give them plenty of time to skedaddle home.

Polly gave Regina a pat, cooing to her that she'd be back soon. The dog was restless and dove under the bed every time a gust of wind caused a fresh batch of acorns to pelt the roof from the overhanging limbs of the giant oak tree in the back of the house.

Picking up her umbrella, Polly set out to drive to her date.

Twelve minutes later she entered Panera Bread and looked around for Sam. Polly knew what he looked like from the pictures he had uploaded to his profile and was about to sit down at a table by the door when she heard her name.

Sam was taller than she expected and much more handsome than his pictures—salt and pepper hair with silver gray at his temples.

"Polly Pringle. Finally." He gave her a peck on the cheek and then guided her to a booth in front of a window. A single red rose, silver paper wrapped around the stem, lay on the table. Sam picked up the flower and extended his hand to her holding the rose. "I feel like we're old friends, Polly, so I'm not going to say it's nice to meet you. Actually, I'm delighted."

"Thank you, Sam. I wish the roses in my garden were this pretty," she said accepting the flower.

"You told me awhile back that you like tea in the afternoon so here you are … a cup of very hot water and four tea bags. Take your pick."

"Oh, I love this lemon ginger. What are you having?"

"Coffee, plain old coffee. Sounds like we're going to be in for a doozy tonight," Sam said. "I also picked out a pastry for us. After all, this is a celebration."

"I've never tasted their desserts—this lemon tart looks yummy," she said her eyes crinkling in the corners as she smiled at Sam. "Why didn't we think of this sooner? Meeting. We certainly have corresponded a lot. Your son, a veterinarian, right?"

"Yes, ma'am. You know that squirrel I talk about?"

"Nugget?"

"Right. I designed a special feeder for him. Carved him a friend out of driftwood and attached it to the tray. It's a double—one side for food, the other for water."

"Does Nugget drink out of it?" Polly asked cutting a piece of the tart with her fork.

"He does. And now my son wants to sell them at his clinic. How about your daughter? Your last message said she had a court case pending. She's concerned about it?" Sam said taking a bite of his tart. "Um, these are good aren't they?"

"To die for, my friend. Sandra always frets over her cases, but she's batting close to a hundred in the winning department."

"I may have to ask that lawyer daughter of yours how to go about applying for a patent on my squirrel feeder," he said chuckling. Taking a sip of his coffee, he looked at Polly and then plunged on with a question. "Polly, I know you like music, especially the symphony, but have you ever been to Branson, Missouri?"

"No, but I've heard about it … and all the stars. I guess some, like Andy Williams, have even built their own theaters."

"Would you like to go? There's a group, a tour bus, in a couple of weeks. There will be other singles like us, so some of the men will share a room. Same for the ladies. I thought about going but it would be so much more fun if you went too. What do you think?"

"Sam, I say let's go for it. Speaking of which, I'd better get on my way. The wind is really whipping up. I'll never get my little Regina out from under the bed."

Polly picked up her rose and glanced out the window. "Oh, my, Sam. Did you see that lightning? That was close."

Polly walked ahead of Sam to the door. Glancing to her left she saw Susan sitting alone, sipping a cup of coffee. She thought about stopping at her table to say hello but decided against it. She looked peeved—her fingers strumming the table.

———

IT HAD BEEN AN hour and still no sight of her date. Susan at first felt hurt, but now she was furious. How dare he leave her drinking coffee alone. She marched out of Panera Bread and drove straight home. She was going to give that Larry person a piece of her mind. As far as trying to arrange another date with her … well, he could forget it. "He'd better not say something came up … I hope you didn't wait too long, Susan dearest," she snarled.
Changing into her slacks, she stopped at her jewelry stand. Removing her pearl-stud earrings and a bracelet, she opened the first drawer to put them in their velvet case.

The drawer was empty.

"What? Where are my diamond earrings, and—"

She jerked open the other five drawers. Empty. All empty. She ran to the telephone beside the bed and dialed 911. She yelled into the phone at the operator that she had been robbed. All of her precious jewelry was gone.

In less than twenty minutes a squad car arrived. Susan met the officer at the door, told him to follow her as she spouted off that she had never been robbed before, and she wanted the culprit thrown in jail. Entering the bedroom, Susan pulled open the empty jewelry drawer and glared at the detective to go and arrest someone.

"What time do you think this happened, Mrs. Armstrong?" Detective Watson asked ignoring her taunting stare.

"Well, I know precisely. I was out of the house between two and four."

"Where were you?"

"I stopped to get a bite to eat at Panera Bread and when I came home my jewelry was gone."

"Your front door lock didn't appear to be jimmied. How do you think the robber got in the house?" Fred asked.

"Maybe ... maybe the back door. I always leave it open." Her voice sharp as she glanced from the empty jewelry cabinet to the detective.

"Have you checked the door since you called us?"

"No."

"By any chance do you have a list of the pieces that are missing?"

"Oh, I can do better than that." Susan stomped back down the stairs to the library, Detective Watson striding in her wake. She pulled open a file drawer, skimmed the contents, and pulled out a large file folder. "Here. It's all here. A picture, a description, and the value. My insurance company also has a copy."

"Do you have any idea who did this?"

"No. No, I don't." She certainly wasn't going to admit to meeting a man online, making a date for coffee, and that he obviously stood her up while she was being vandalized.

Chapter 41

July 14, Wednesday, 4:00 P.M.

HARRI WAS TRYING, UNSUCCESSFULLY, not to show Kelly how concerned and scared he was becoming as every minute passed. He was mad at himself for stalling the ransom payment until tomorrow. Mad at Fisher for suggesting it. He had the money in his bank account ready to transfer. He had set up a special account whereby he could access the funds 24/7 and complete a wire transfer at any time of day or night. He had logged into this account several times just to make sure the balance was correct.

The caller didn't say what time or how the instructions would arrive only that it would arrive. For some reason, Harri thought the man might change his mind—call today. Maybe something was wrong. He should have asked to talk to Vicky, be sure he really did have her, but the man never gave him a chance. He had hoped Vicky would be home by now.

The phone rang and he jumped to answer it but Kelly beat him to it. She stood listening.

"Kelly, tell Carol you'll call her—"

Kelly waved him off. "Thank you, Captain Salinas. Do you want to talk to my dad? ... I'll tell him."

She hung up the phone and turned to Harri. "He called to say his detectives were still looking in the Astor Park vicinity. They talked to several people with trailers but nothing yet. Same story as when Liz dropped my phone off earlier. He was going into a meeting and said he'd call you back. He also said there could be a problem."

"What?"

"The wildfires."

Harri sighed, looked out the window, hands on his hips when the front doorbell rang. He ran to answer it—Kelly behind him. He yanked the door open. A UPS delivery man stood on the other side of the screen door holding a large carton.

"Hello, sir. I have a package for you."

"Dad, why would he send a box?" Kelly whispered squeezing in beside him to see through the screen.

"I don't know."

The delivery man handed Harri an electronic clipboard and a special pen indicating where he should sign. "Thanks, sir." He handed the carton to Harri and turned to leave.

"Wait a minute," Harri yelled after him. "This isn't mine. It's addressed to Polly Pringle. My name is Brookfield."

The man trotted back and looked at the box. "Sorry, sir, but the address—"

"It's my address," Harri said raising his voice, "but Mrs. Pringle is two doors down. The address is wrong."

"Oh, I see. Sorry."

The man in the brown suit picked up the box, returned to his van and backed up. Harri shut the door, his heart racing as he leaned back against the doorjamb.

"Dad, do you think he, the man who has mom, is playing a game with us?"

"I hope not, Kel."

The doorbell rang again and Harri jumped back, jerking the door open.

"Sorry to bother you again, sir, but Mrs. Pringle doesn't seem to be home. Because you've already signed for the package could you add that you accepted it for Mrs. Pringle? I'll leave it here, (delete "," after "here") if you don't mind giving it to her."

"Fine, fine—just give it to me."

The delivery man put the carton in Harri's hands and ran back to his truck as the Brookfield door slammed shut.

"Dad, do you think we should open it ... to be sure it's not about mom?"

Harri turned the carton over, breathed a heavy sigh and handed it to Kelly tapping the return address for her to read. The carton was sent from the Regional Director, Quilts of Valor.

Father and daughter returned to the kitchen and checked the equipment lined up on the counter: Kelly's cell, next to Harri's cell and laptop. They had set their email accounts to sound an alert if a message hit the inbox in any one of their various accounts. Harri had set up a shortcut on his laptop to access his special bank account.

All they could do was wait.

The wind swirled—debris hitting the side of the house and the windows.

Chapter 42

———

July 14, Wednesday, 7:32 P.M.

VICTORIA SWUNG HER LEGS over the side of the bed. Did she hear Richard's car return or was it the wind? She wondered if he had sent the wire-transfer information to Harri and if he did, did Harri wire the two million dollars?

The front door opened, banging against the wall from the force of the wind. She heard him shut the door, heard the clatter of pans, then his footsteps approaching her door. He fumbled with the padlock and pushed the door open. As before, he stood in the doorway looking at her, then turned back to the kitchen.

"Come on out. I bought groceries for dinner."

Victoria tiptoed out of the bedroom. Several bags were on the table including a bottle of wine. He caught her looking at the wine.

"You'll be leaving soon, so—"

He shrugged leaving the sentence hanging in the air. He walked past her and into the bedroom. She heard the shower running as she removed the groceries from the brown plastic bags—box of linguine, jar of spaghetti sauce, an onion and a small container of mushrooms.

"Looks like a feast," she said softly, emptying the rest of the bags with prepared lettuce for a salad, two bottles of dressing—blue cheese and Italian, as well as a baguette of French bread, the slices smeared with garlic butter, and some freshly grated Parmesan cheese. She put the Dove bars in the freezer compartment of the refrigerator. He had put a pot of water on the stove to boil for the pasta.

Returning in fresh clothes, jeans and a black tank-top, he set to dicing the onion. "The shower was cold. You never said. Hand me the Italian dressing will you? Please?" He glanced at her then quickly looked away.

She did as he asked, not replying to his mention of the cold shower water, and watched him put a few tablespoons of the dressing in the pot of water and in the large frying pan heating on the stove. He dumped the onions and the mushrooms into the pan.

"I've never seen Italian dressing used that way," she said finding her voice.

"You pick up all kinds of tricks in the inmate's cooking school. See what you can find for dishes. Oh, and there are some candles in that first cupboard. We'll pretend we're marooned on an island, shipwrecked due to a storm." He smiled at her, but she didn't see the hurt in his eyes. Her back was to him as she wiped out two water glasses and set them on the table.

Handing her the wooden spoon he was using to stir the onions and mushrooms, his hand brushed hers. They both looked up— surprised by the electricity that raced through their arms.

Victoria turned down the burner and stirred the onion mixture, her heart beating wildly, her breath stuck in her chest.

Richard lit the three candles in small jars on the table and retrieved four more from the cupboard. He placed them on the coffee table and end tables next to the couch and chair, lighting them as he went. Grabbing the corkscrew he set about opening the wine bottle pouring some of the deep-red liquid into the two glasses. The water hissed in the pot and he emptied the carton of linguine into the bubbling water, lowered the heat. The air was filled with tension ... working so close ... the erratic beats of their hearts.

Victoria set the table and put the lettuce in a bowl. The cheese and dressings were already on the table. Moving around she made sure she kept the table between them. She couldn't stop herself from wanting this dinner to last for a long time ... forever. Shaking her head free of this thought, she turned her back to him, wondering if he felt what she was feeling.

How did this happen? Not more than a few months ago he was in California—in prison. She was in Florida in a prison not of her making, but none-the-less a prison. She had not been able to accept the circumstances when they left San Francisco, to begin life again with her new name. But, this man had torn down her prison walls.

Victoria closed her eyes. *If only we were marooned on an island, it would be—"* She opened her eyes, wiped a tear away, and noticed the front door was not bolted shut.

"Dinner's ready," Richard announced, handing her a glass of wine. He tapped his glass to hers without looking at her and quickly sat down.

Did she see a tremor in his hand or was it her imagination?

Their dinner conversation came in fits and starts. He asked about her parents and had it been hard to relocate.

"Harri and I lied to Kelly about our parents saying mine had moved to London because of business and Harri's to Alaska. We stopped talking about them. We begged the marshals to let her keep her first name, and in time she forgot Babcock and became a Brookfield. I went from Vivien to Victoria and Harri was previously Herbert Babcock."

"It must have been hard—starting over."

"The sudden move was the initial reason I didn't look for a job, but then I … I withdrew … withdrew from life. Over the years I questioned myself … why couldn't I adjust to the situation?" Victoria sipped her wine, looked up at him and asked about what his life was like in San Francisco, how he fell in with the man she called evil.

Her question opened a floodgate of emotion as he told her of his childhood, growing up in one foster home after another. But along the way, one of his foster mothers saw him drawing. She bought him paints and brought home used paper from where she worked. Later she introduced him to an established artist who took him under his wing and instructed him much as a master trains an apprentice. But the woman died, the artist moved away. He worked at odd jobs but nothing stuck. Pit Bull picked him up off the streets one night and fed him.

He told Victoria his real name was Robert Steele and then revealed the story of how he came to her … and fixed dinner this night.

Relating the memories of his past to Victoria, and the truth about why he was in Florida, had a cathartic effect. He was breathing easier, stopped the pacing, now, at the end of his story, a story he had never told before. Victoria cleared the table—she hadn't touched her dinner, and Richard poured the last of the wine in their glasses.

"I have something to show you ... I wasn't going to ... but—"

Richard walked to the bedroom closet and retrieved a tube on the top shelf. Back in the living room, he motioned to her to sit in the easy chair. As she sat down he opened the tube and withdrew a roll of heavy paper.

"You asked to see what I was sketching when we first met in the bookstore." Unrolling the heavy art paper and holding it up for her to see, Victoria's hand flew to her mouth, her eyes opening wide.

"Richard, it's ... it's beautiful. The colors in the scarf, my eyes—"

"I tried to capture how you looked that day. How I saw you. Your eyes soft, accepting."

He put the painting on the couch and pulled out the second painting, hesitating before unrolling it, and then continued, holding it open, his fingers quivered, as she saw herself lying on the bed after he had made love to her. She was covered with a white sheet, but he had painted the form of her body, the sheet tucked tightly around her.

"I ... I don't know what to say. You captured the beauty of that afternoon."

"Your beauty, Victoria."

He rolled the paintings together, returned them to the tube and threw it on the counter. Victoria stood, picked up their wine glasses, handing him his. Standing face to face, they looked into each other's eyes and he slowly lowered his lips to hers. The kiss deepened. Their breathing became labored. He took her glass and set it on the table next to his, then wrapped her in his arms, tight, tighter, so he could feel every curve of her body melting into his.

"Richard ... make love to me ... one last time ... please ... I love you," she whispered.

His eyes closed, he shook his head from side to side ... "Victoria, don't ask me ..."

He picked her up, walked to the bedroom carefully laying her on the bed, knowing the moment they were stealing would have to last a lifetime.

They moved in slow motion—tasting, touching—this moment to remember the look and feel of their bodies, their voices murmuring their love for one another. Her body rose to accept his as they clung to each other for the last time.

———

VICTORIA SLEPT IN RICHARD'S arms. He carefully pulled away and got out of bed. He looked down at her for a moment and then tiptoed into the living room and turned on his computer. Waiting for the machine to finish the start-up routine, he picked up his wine glass, took a sip, then sat in front of the laptop. He rented a ten-minute email account under an alias and typed the wire-transfer instructions for Harri to follow.

He clicked the send button.

He canceled the email account.

Logged out of the website.

And, turned off the computer.

Chapter 43

BULL PACED FROM WINDOW to door of his motel room, back and forth, back and forth, stopping only for another swallow of his boilermaker. The more he drank the more he paced. The more he paced the more agitated he became, constantly muttering to himself. "That bastard Babcock. Living all these years under palm trees while I'm hiding, looking over my shoulder. Looking and wondering if the man next to me is going to pull a gun, arrest me, or worse, maybe one of my guys turning on me."

Scratching his ample belly, he poured himself another drink. "Haven't heard from Razor. He must have the money by now. He's not answering my calls. Maybe he's run off with that Mrs. Babcock. Running off with my money."

He peeked out the curtain as a bolt of lightning hit off in the distance followed by a thunderclap.

"It would be a good night to take Babcock out. Nobody hearin nothin—just thunder. No gunshot. Finish him off then I don't have to worry no more about him testifying."

He laughed at how funny that sounded. "Can't testify if he can't talk."

Bull checked his revolver, making sure the clip was loaded and left the motel. He'd driven by Babcock's house a few times, always late at night. He passed an occasional car but people weren't venturing out fearing the approaching hurricane. Driving down the deserted streets, he formulated his attack. He knew that Babcock had a daughter. *Can't let her see me. That brat of his better stay away if she knows what's good for her.*

A gust of wind rocked his car. He gripped the wheel tighter. Lightning danced around him followed by cracks of thunder. He turned onto Babcock's street just as a bolt of lightning knocked out the electricity. The street went black. The houses silhouetted with each lightning strike followed by black on black.

Bull parked alongside a conservation area four houses down from Babcock's. Snaking through the backyards to Babcock's house, not knowing when lightning was going to strike next, he hugged the shrubbery. He crouched against a tall bush behind the next-door neighbor's house, catching his breath, deciding the best way to get into the house. *The back door will more than likely be locked.* He chuckled. A locked door never stopped him before. He was an expert at picking locks. He stooped, creeping to Babcock's back door when suddenly a bolt of lightning lit up the sky. He dove behind a bush waiting for the thunder to roll by. He didn't notice the curtain move ever so slightly in the neighbor's kitchen window.

———

MILDRED DIDN'T LIKE lightning and was scurrying around the house—window to window. The last bolt of lightning illuminated Polly's and Vicky's backyards but especially her own sandwiched between the two.

She gasped, her hands flying to her mouth. In the shadows she saw a large man. She was sure of it. Racing to the telephone she stumbled over a kitchen chair. Crying out in pain and fright, she got to her feet and grabbed for the telephone on the wall. Her fingers quivered as she withdrew the small flashlight from her apron pocket. Trying to hold the wobbly beam steady, she dialed 911.

"911. What's your emergency?"

"A man, a big man, is creeping around the back of my house," she whispered. "He's at my neighbor's. I think he's going to rob us. Hurry."

"Please speak up. I can barely hear you. Your name?"

"Mildred Porter. Please, hurry. Hurry."

"An officer is on his way. What's your neighbor's name?"

"Brookfield. Harri Brookfield."

On Nova Road a squad car screeched into a U-turn and headed to the Pelican Bay development. The officer had driven by the Brookfield residence not more than fifteen minutes before. He called the dispatcher and asked her to immediately inform Captain Salinas about the 911 call and the address.

——

LENNY WAS BEING interrogated by two of Manny's detectives. They had already talked to Billy, who was street smart and clammed up the minute the officers said they had a few questions for him. He insisted he never heard of Herbert Babcock, Robert Steele, or Richard Stiles. Sure he knew the name Brookfield. They lived two doors down from his customer, Mrs. Pringle. When he was taken to a holding cell, he demanded to see a lawyer.

Lenny, on the other hand, said he knew Robert Steele. Steele was his friend, but everyone called him Razor. He never heard of Herbert Babcock or Richard Stiles, but he knew Brookfield's name because he was a neighbor of the lady Billy and he worked for.

One of the detectives was called out of the interrogation room by an officer who handed him a report. Seems Lenny had an account on Billy's computer for a dating site. They found his name but the profile described an older man, late forties, and the picture didn't match. He and a woman, who went by the handle of Rainbow, had set up a date. The date occurred the same date and time as a jewelry robbery of a home on A1A, overlooking the ocean.

While Lenny was left in the interrogation room, an officer obtained a warrant to search Billy's trailer. The two detectives took the warrant and sped over to the trailer park. Searching the trailer they quickly found a bag of jewelry in a suitcase. They continued to search and found a revolver in the bottom of a chest of drawers covered with socks. Finding nothing else of interest they returned to the department. The gun was given to forensics to check for prints.

The detectives checked the pieces they found in the bag against the list of jewelry that had been stolen. The items matched. They knew they had their man—fingerprints should tell them which one—Billy or Lenny. They played a hunch and showed the suitcase first to Billy. He claimed it was Lenny's. Next they showed the case to Lenny. He said the case was his but he didn't know how the jewelry got there. The officers said they thought it would be a good idea if Lenny spent the night in a cell on Florida's dime, but first a U.S. Marshal wanted to have a word with him.

Manny and Liz were in the conference room discussing what they had found out so far from Billy. They were sure the detectives had solved the jewelry heist but they were no closer to finding Mrs. Brookfield. A fresh carafe of coffee was on the table—it looked like they were about to pull an all-nighter.

Manny leaned over the table to answer the phone. The dispatcher relayed the message from the officer in route to check on a 911 call. Manny instantly stood up and asked to be immediately patched through to the officer. He looked at his watch then over at Liz. He shouted orders to the officer on how he should proceed when he arrived at the Pelican Bay development.

"Block the street—both ends. No sirens. Cut the lights. I'm on my way."

———

FISHER WAS STILL INTERROGATING Lenny when an officer ran into the room.

"Captain Salinas wants to see you right away. He's in the car out front."

Lenny put up a fuss saying they couldn't hold him, but Fisher told the officer to put Lenny in a holding cell for the night. Then he rushed out of the building and climbed into the back seat of Manny's SUV. Manny's foot hit the gas pedal and they sped out of the parking area. Liz, sitting in front with Manny, quickly filled Fisher in about the 911 call.

"Maybe Robert Steele has gone to Brookfield's to kill him," Fisher said, hanging onto the handle over the door as the car swerved around the corner.

Chapter 44

July 14, Wednesday, 9:32 P.M.

"DAD," KELLY SCREAMED. "There's a message alert on your laptop."

Harri ran to the kitchen following the beam of his flashlight. Laying the flashlight on the counter, his fingers began flying over the keyboard to access the message. The subject: "Your turn." It was addressed to Harri but the *From* field was blank.

> "Wire the money to the account below. Do this in the next
> fifteen minutes—I presume you are ready and waiting. Once
> the account acknowledges receipt of the transfer, you will
> receive the location where you can pick up your wife."

"Kelly, write down this number," Harri said pointing to the screen. "Can you see it?"

"Yes, yes." Kelly carefully wrote the account number on the notepad beside her dad's laptop.

"Read it back to me … that's right … that's right." Harri immediately logged into his bank and the special account he had set up.

"Okay. Kelly, read the account numbers to me," Harri asked struggling to maintain control over his racing heart. "Take your time."

Kelly's hand was shaking so hard she had to put the notepad down on the counter in order to hold the flashlight to see the numbers. She read them slowly and then repeated them at her father's request. The numbers checked.

The bank's website displayed the message: "Do you want to go ahead with the above transfer?"

Harri clicked "YES."

A warning message instantly appeared on the computer screen: "No battery. Plug computer into a power source."

The screen turned black.

"No. No! Did the transfer go through?" Harri shouted at the screen. He pulled at the power cord. The plug dangled from his fingers. He hadn't plugged it in since the night before. The computer had been on all day in case the kidnapper sent the instructions by email. The battery was dead.

Kelly put her arms around her dad leaning her head against his arm. The candles on the kitchen table and the candles on the counter continued to burn brightly.

"Dad, we won't know where mom is. The man who has mom won't know our computer is down. Maybe the transfer didn't go through."

Chapter 45

—

July 14, Wednesday, 10:10 P.M.

BULL STUMBLED AS HE EMERGED from the bush by Brookfield's back door. He saw a dim flicker in the window.

"Damn. Candles. He must be in there. No way I'm gonna surprise him."

Sticking close to the house in case of another streak of lightning, he made his way to the front muttering every step of the way about his lousy luck. Maybe he could rush him through the front door.

The dark, coupled with his alcohol intake, hampered his footing. He cussed each step slipping on the wet grass, as a squad car, lights out, slowly rolled by the house.

"Shit. I'll have to make this fast." Bull could hear himself breathing hard—mouth open, vision blurred. "He's leaving. Didn't see me. Why's he driving with no lights?"

Bull looked around, waiting to see if the car returned. It didn't. Thinking it safe, he stepped out of the bushes at the same time a second squad car rolled by without headlights. Fear crept up his spine. Fight or flight? He chose the latter.

Turning around, he dashed to the backyard, his feet again sliding on the slippery grass, bushes reaching out clawing at his trousers. Through three more backyards he ran, finally lurching to his car. Fumbling with the keys, he opened the car door, started the engine, turned on his lights, and sped down the street. Suddenly a squad car straddling the street appeared in his headlights. He swerved around the corner, then another. Unfamiliar with the development, he realized too late that he had turned onto a dead-end street. Screeching to a stop, he jumped out of the car and began running. Two officers approached in hot pursuit yelling at him to stop. Bull switched direction. The officers closed in and tackled him, wrestling him to the ground. He had no opportunity to draw his gun, or time to throw it in the bushes before the officers grabbed it.

"This is a mistake. You scared me. I'm lost," Bull cried out.

"You're also drunk, mister."

The officers from the second squad car held the shrieking man in their high beams. Bull immediately calmed down, assuming an air of thankfulness that the officers found him before he hurt himself.

"Can you lead me out of this maze?" he asked, now on his feet supported by an officer on either side.

"Let's see what you register on the breathalyzer. Then we'll talk." The officers escorted him to their car, Bull stumbling along between them.

"Hey, Fred. Look what we found under his front seat." The officer held up a large bag filled with a white substance. "I think this guy has some explaining to do."

"What? That's not mine. I don't know how it got there. I've been framed," he screamed.

"Sure, sure. That's what they all say." Fred said.

Manny, Fisher, and Liz pulled up, parking behind the two squad cars. Seeing a large man in the headlights suddenly sit down on the ground, they quickly joined the group.

Manny held back to answer his cell. The desk sergeant had received a call from Harrison Brookfield. His laptop was dead and he urgently needed to have access to a computer.

"Tell Harri to meet me at the department. Tell him I'll be back shortly to set him up."

Manny trotted to catch up with Fisher and Liz.

"That's not Steele," Liz said. "This guy doesn't look like him or Stiles."

Chapter 46

———

July 14, Wednesday, 10:53 P.M.

LEAVING THE CHUBBY, SQUEALING prisoner with his officers, Manny waited for Fisher and Liz to join him in the car, turned on his high beams and left Pelican Bay Development cloaked in darkness. The wind buffeted the car. Manny snapped on the weather station.

"This is WROD 1230 weather alert.

We have just received a severe weather bulletin for all of northern and central Florida.

Tornado and severe lightning warnings have just been issued. A tornado was spotted east of Orlando. Rotations are popping up on Doppler radar indicating possible tornado activity in Orange and Volusia Counties.

The Category 2 hurricane, with sustained winds at over ninety-six miles per hour, is moving slowly through the Gulf and is estimated to make landfall sometime in the early morning hours. Due to its erratic path, it could make landfall anywhere from Alabama to the panhandle of Florida, or all of north-west Florida.

To make matters worse, the red-flag warning issued yesterday due to the months of drought suffered across Florida is still in effect. You are advised to keep a watchful eye out for fires and report them to your local fire department immediately. Already firefighters are stretched thin responding to calls from lightning-ignited flames eating up the dry underbrush of leaves and pine needles.

Highway I-95 between Port Orange, Route 421, and Ormond Beach, Route 40, are closed due to the fast-moving fires.

Stayed tuned to WROD for late-breaking news on our weather conditions."

———

THE DESK SERGEANT called to Manny, as he, Liz, and Fisher hustled into the DBPD, a gust of wind pushing them through the doorway.

"Harrison Brookfield is in the first conference room." The desk sergeant called out and then quickly sat down to take another emergency call.

Manny turned down the hall followed closely by Liz and Fisher. They found Harri pacing, Kelly leaning against the wall. They both shouted at the same time.

"He emailed the instructions!"

"Sorry, Dad."

"I followed the instructions. Kelly and I checked the account number twice. It matched. It was perfect."

"You did good. So, what's the matter?" Manny asked.

"I don't know if it went through. My laptop died."

"Come on upstairs, Harri—" Manny looked at the group standing around him. "Harri, you and Kelly follow me. I'll set you up on a computer. Stitch, come with us. Fisher stay here. I'll have the officers bring our new drunken prisoner into the interrogation room. Hope he has a good reason to be sneaking around the Brookfield house. Ask the desk sergeant to show you where the coffee is."

"What's this about a man sneaking around our house?" Harri asked. "We just left there."

"Come on, I'll fill you in," Manny said hustling out of the conference room. Not bothering with the elevator, he headed for the stairs. Liz followed as Fisher headed to the front lobby.

On the third floor, Manny steered Harri to a desk with a computer overlooking the lobby below. Kelly sat next to her father watching as he accessed the internet. They all looked out the glass as a commotion developed in the lobby. The two officers who had transported their new prisoner in handcuffs continued screaming that he had been framed. Both Harri and Kelly stood up so they could see who was causing the ruckus.

"Oh, my God! It's him!" Harri cried out sinking into the chair then immediately jumping up to look down again through the glass, blood draining from his face.

"Dad, what's the matter?" Kelly asked.

"Get Fisher! Hurry, get Fisher." Harri's voice strangled in his throat. He again sank into the chair, leaned forward, elbows on his knees, his head dropping down between his legs.

Manny and Liz locked eyes. Manny nodded to her to get Fisher as he picked up the desk phone and requested a bottle of cold water. "Fast!"

Kelly knelt beside her father. "What do you mean, it's him?" she whispered.

"Wait. Wait for Fisher," he mumbled gulping for air.

The elevator door opened and Fisher and Liz hurried to Harri's side. Fisher put a hand on his shoulder, squatted to see Harri's face.

"What is it, Harrison?"

Harri lifted his head but continued to support his body with his elbows.

"That man."

"What man?"

"That man screaming in the lobby."

"Go on."

"It's him."

"Who?"

"The man who killed my partner."

Fisher ran to the staircase and down the three fights, his feet pounding on the steel treads. Manny was on his heels. Fisher yelled commands over his shoulder as he ran. Get that man's prints and send them to the Fed's office in San Francisco. Tell them that Marshal Ken Fisher wants the prints checked against the set on file they found eleven years ago in the murder case of Frank Pitman. I'll meet you in the interrogation room."

Slamming through the staircase door to the first floor, Fisher jogged to question the prisoner as Manny hustled to get his forensic team and to place a call to WITSEC, San Francisco.

The desk sergeant watched the two lawmen dash in different directions as a weather bulletin lit up her screen.

"A major fire is burning out of control along the St. John's River and is approaching Route 40. Evacuations have been ordered. The highway is closed in both directions."

"Dad. Dad. You have to check your email. Maybe the kidnapper received the money. Maybe he's sent a message where mom is."

Harri looked at Kelly. She shook his arm. "Now, Dad! Now!"

Harri slowly straightened up, put his fingers on the keyboard and typed the address to access his email account, his fingers barely moving. A random list of websites appeared on the screen—he typed the wrong address. Gathering strength, he retyped the address and entered his username and password. There was one message in his inbox.

"Subject: Your wife

Wait for her on the dirt road off of Route 40, Astor Park. East side of the bridge."

Chapter 47

July 14, Wednesday, 11:03 P.M.

A SPEAR OF LIGHTNING hitting a transformer lit the sky, followed by an explosive crack of thunder shaking the small trailer on its cement block pillars.

Richard and Victoria's heads snapped up, their eyes fixed on the small window in the living room. They heard sirens in the distance, thunderclaps, and more lightning streaking across the sky.

Richard stepped out the front door. The air was heavy with smoke. He saw flames through the trees. Shutting the door, he knelt in front of Victoria. His strong hands clutched hers lying folded in her lap.

"Victoria, we've run out of time. I ask you again, plead with you, come away with me—the Caribbean, South France, wherever you say. We have money—you can start a business if you like—"

"And you will paint. Richard, you have so much to give, to say through your brushes filled with color. Your charcoals are exquisite. My sweet, sweet, man—you must paint. I know in my heart you will."

"Only if you're with me—if not my desire to paint will wither and die."

"I can't, Richard. You will always hold a special place in my heart. A place that will be locked tight. Maybe in time I'll open it ... when I dare to think of you—your touch, your lips on mine. But only when I'm alone, because the memory of you will be written on my face for all to read. And, I can't let that happen. I will not hurt Harri again. Who would have thought that events so many years ago would bring me the passion of my life ... I have to go."

Tears welled up in their eyes. He lifted her folded hands to his lips, kissing them with tenderness. A tear meandered down his cheek falling on her fingers.

Another lightning bolt struck nearby followed by several claps of thunder that again shook the trailer. Victoria wiped the tear from his cheek as he wiped hers away. He enfolded her in his arms pressing his lips to her cheek, forehead, each tear-filled eye, then pushed her to the door.

"Hurry—run toward the sirens."

"What about you?" she screamed. She stood ... frozen.

"Go. Go!" he pushed her out the door and watched her run up the dirt path ... she turned to look at him ... and ... then she was gone, enveloped in the thick, black smoke.

Chapter 48

THE SMOKE BURNED VICKY'S eyes as she ran down the path away from the trailer. She didn't know where the path led but when it came to a dirt road, she turned to her right seeing flames overhead to her left licking the top of a pine tree, but she soon realized the fire was advancing toward her. Keeping her eyes shut but for very narrow slits, she reversed direction hearing sirens and men shouting.

She heard herself scream, "Harri. Harri. Help!" The smoke searing her lungs, she stumbled and fell. Crawling on the ground, she tried to stand, but she couldn't get her footing. "Harri," she whispered. Suddenly she felt herself being lifted, the arms of the man tightened around her as he ran toward lights in the distance. He continued to run, the lights becoming brighter as he broke through the smoke.

"Mom. Mom."

Who was it? A girl. A girl was calling her. The man holding her released her into the arms of another firefighter.

"Ma'am, it's all right. You're safe now."

Someone took hold of her hand.

"Harri?" Her voice so weak she could barely say his name.

"Mom. It's me. Kelly."

Vicky buried her face in the fireman's chest as he ran away from the approaching flames.

"I'm so sorry," she whispered, the smoke stinging her throat.

The man laid Vicky on the ground and dashed back into the smoke.

Kelly dropped to her knees clutching her mother's hand to her heart, tears cascading down her cheeks. "Help. Help!" Kelly screamed.

Vicky turned her head to her. "Kelly, my beautiful Kelly. I love you."

When Liz saw Kelly kneeling on the ground beside a woman, she ran to the nearest fireman for help. He immediately radioed for an ambulance. In minutes the wailing of the EMT's siren approached the roadblock and stopped.

The medics ran down the pavement.

"Here ... please ... help my mom," Kelly cried out.

The men turned down the dirt road and ran to Kelly and her mother.

Vicky's eyes were closed. "Is she conscious?"

"She was just talking to me," Kelly whispered.

The medics gently lifted Vicky onto the stretcher.

"No, no. Don't leave me." Vicky could only mouth the words.

"I'm here, Mom. I'm here." Kelly held tight to her mother's hand as they hustled as fast as they could up the dirt road to the EMT van.

Chapter 49

———

July 15, Thursday, 7:00 A.M.

MORNING DAWNED WITH A clear blue sky over central Florida, a slight breeze from west to north-east chasing the remnants of the storm up the east coast and out to sea. The hurricane veered north in the early morning hours into Alabama and Georgia, grazing Florida. The outer bands brought torrents of rain helping to dampen the wildfires.

Vicky felt a familiar hand as she opened her eyes. Kelly was sitting in a chair beside her hospital bed, her head lying on the bed's blanket, eyes closed. The room was still.

Vicky tried to speak but her throat was constricted and she winced in pain.

Kelly raised her head, sat up feeling the pressure of Vicky's hand jerk. "Don't talk," she whispered. "The doctor said its best not to. Your throat is slightly burned from the smoke. You'll be okay in a few days, at least to whisper." She smiled lifting her mother's hand to her lips. "How're you feeling?"

Vicky smiled and nodded, giving a thumbs-up gesture.

The door opened and a woman walked in.

Kelly looked up and smiled. "Mom, this is Elizabeth Stitchway. She's a private investigator dad hired to help find you."

Elizabeth stepped forward. "Hi, Mrs. Brookfield," Liz said squeezing her hand in greeting.

Vicky mouthed, "Call me Vicky." Smiling, she squeezed Liz's hand back.

"Captain Salinas, Daytona Beach Police, is out in the hall talking to your doctor," Liz said. "He's hoping you can lead us to the trailer later this morning, or whenever you feel up to it. It's important you take us there as soon as possible. The captain wants to find the man who kidnapped you, but he may have been killed in the fire."

Vicky again squeezed Liz's hand, nodded vigorously that she wanted to go. She gingerly sat up in the bed swinging her legs over the side.

"Whoa, not yet, Mom. Let's get the doctor's okay first."

The door opened and the doctor entered the room with Manny on his heels.

"Well, look at this," Dr. Tredwell said. Liz and Kelly backed out of the way and walked to the other side of the bed. "You sure look a lot better than you did last night. Breathe as normally as you can but stop when your throat hurts." He placed his stethoscope on her chest then her back. "Lungs sound fine. Now let's take a look at that throat. Open your mouth but don't say ah," he said smiling at her. "Not too bad, Vicky. I'll give you a shot for the pain and some liquid medication that will help your throat. You'll have to stay on a liquid diet for a few days—soft foods."

"What do you think, doc. If she says she's up to it, do we have your okay for a quick trip to see if she can locate that trailer?" Manny asked.

"Mom, this is Captain Salinas. He's been working your case with Liz and the marshal," Kelly said, once again taking hold of her hand. She saw fear cross her mother's face. "It's okay. So much has happened since you've been missing. But the good news is you're finally safe," Kelly whispered.

Vicky raised her eyebrows.

"I know about WITSEC, Mom, but I want to hear more once your throat doesn't hurt."

Vicky closed her eyes and let out a shallow sigh, her shoulders relaxing.

"Do you think you're up to going with the captain, Vicky," the doctor asked.

Vicky nodded, yes, squeezing Kelly's hand twice.

"Okay, Captain, but keep it as short as you can," the doctor said. "Give her an hour so the medication can start working on her throat. I believe Kelly brought a change of clothes."

"Sure did," Kelly said beaming at her mom.

"Liz, lets you and I clear out of here so Mrs. Brookfield can get changed," Manny said.

"I want to go with her, Captain," Kelly said gripping her mother's hand.

"Not a problem, young lady. Liz and I will put Mrs. Brookfield's things in your car when we leave. Liz and I have some phone calls to make—we'll meet you out front."

In less than an hour, Vicky was ready to be released and eager to leave the hospital. Kelly zipped up the rolling suitcase, grabbed the handle as well as the bag of scorched, smoky, men's clothing her mother had been wearing.

Vicky took hold of Kelly's hand. Looking into her daughter's eyes, she mouthed, "Harri?"

"Oh … well … he had quite a night. I'll tell you about it later. He said he'd see you at home. He had a research meeting of some kind this morning."

Kelly saw her mother's shoulders slump. She quickly took both of her mom's hands in hers, lifted them, and planted a quick kiss on her knuckles.

Vicky's heart raced visualizing a similar scene hours earlier but with a different person. Looking into Kelly's eyes, her lips formed the words: "I love you."

"I love you too, Mom."

Vicky squeezed her hand gently and smiled, her eyes tearing.

Chapter 50

—

HOT, STICKY AIR CLUNG to central Florida in the wake of Hurricane Bonnie. Returning to Astor Park, the squad car passed a couple of firemen tamping down some remaining hot spots, puffs of smoke escaping and curling above a carpet of smoldering forest debris.

Liz and Manny walked on either side of Vicky, Kelly following, as they slowly made their way along the dirt road off of Route 40. Vicky turned down one path but it ended at a wooden shanty burned to the ground leaving only a skeleton of what was once a cabin.

They came to another path and tentatively began following the weed-infested dirt. Vicky stopped abruptly, reaching for Liz's hand, holding it in a death grip. Ahead was a mobile home, a trailer. The trailer, or what was left of it. Flames had blackened the outside and appeared to have raced through the inside. Wisps of smoke curled from under the scorched aluminum siding. Vicky turned to Manny. She whispered, "Here."

Manny walked ahead, poked his head in the door, looking around the inside. He carefully entered the gutted carcass, walking through to the rear. A wooden chair was burned leaving only the seat. An upholstered couch and chair were charred and still smoldering. The paneling was burned away to the metal frame of the trailer.

He retraced his steps and joined the women standing outside the door.

"Nothing in there but burned furniture. I didn't see a body," he said looking at Vicky.

Vicky stepped up to the door, still holding Liz's hand, pulling her along. She shook her head at Kelly not to follow. "Wait."

"Be careful," Manny said. "It's still hot."

Vicky entered looking to her right into the kitchen. The wood cabinets were gutted. She turned and looked to her left taking a couple of steps into what had served as a small living room, a couch cushion continued to smolder. She picked up a charred leg of a chair—the rest of the chair had burned away. With the leg, she lifted the corner of a cushion, then the next cushion, then the big cushion of an easy chair. Underneath laid a heavy cardboard mailing tube preserved by the large cushion. Dropping Liz's hand, Vicky carefully removed the tube.

She turned to Liz. "You keep," she whispered. "Give me … two months." She put the tube in Liz's hand, wrapping Liz's fingers around the tube. Holding Liz's other hand, she stepped into what was the bedroom. Staring at the bed, Vicky's pulse raced, but she quickly turned away to the closet. The door was gone. She let go of Liz's hand, leaned into the space, covering her nose from the stench of smoke. The case was gone. The case filled with Richard's prison sketches was gone.

Vicky took one last look around. She glanced at Liz and nodded that she had seen enough. They carefully made their way to the front door and stepped outside. Manny was poking around in the charred underbrush looking for any sign of the man who had held Vicky captive. Kelly stood looking at the water—the water in the picture her mother had emailed to her.

Vicky strode several yards toward what she now knew was the St. John's River. She turned, looked back at the smoldering trailer, moved a couple of steps to her right lining up with the bedroom window where she had taken the picture. Then she took several strides almost to the water's edge and stopped.

Liz saw what she was doing and followed behind as did Kelly. Standing in back of Vicky, Liz said, "I could have sworn there was a rowboat tied up to the dock in the picture you sent to Kelly. No sign of it though. Must have burned up with that tree. Still …"

Vicky smiled, closed her eyes, and looked skyward. She turned back to Liz and her daughter.

"Go now," she whispered.

Chapter 51

———

Four Weeks Later

THE QUILTERS HAD BEEN idle for a month. Polly finally rescued the new quilt pieces from the box, the box which was nearly returned because of the wrong address. But thankfully Harri Brookfield saw the error and accepted the carton for Polly Pringle.

With lots of gossip to share, no one was going to miss out on the start of a new quilt and surely Kelly would fill them in on her mother's ordeal. The girls arrived early and friendly chatter filled Polly's dining room as each quilter removed the equipment from her tote necessary for her section—scissors, needles, some with thimbles and some not.

The top of the quilt featured beautiful appliqués on soft white cotton woven with a high thread count. The appliqués bloomed with bouquets of flowers in shades of purple, pale lavender, and hues of pinks. The leaves were sage to apple green and held together with bows of pale yellow at the base of each bouquet.

The director of the Quilts of Valor included a picture of an Army lieutenant sitting next to her little three-year-old daughter. The soldier had lost a leg in Iraq. Because the director liked the way Polly's group had stitched the top to bottom with colored thread, she suggested this quilt, with the colorful appliqués, might lend itself nicely to the same treatment. The quilters agreed, picking out the thread that matched their section from the bowl of spools on Polly's buffet.

"Who's the man in your backyard," Mildred asked. She was sporting a new pink-and-white striped house dress with a green apron.

THE PAINTER | 193

"That's Sam. I told you about him, Mildred—the man I've been dating," Polly answered, securing a knot on the end of her thread.

"Dating? More than once?" Susan asked looking up.

"Several times. He's really nice."

"What's he doing in the yard?" Mildred asked, pulling her needle filled with violet thread through her first stitch.

"He's installing a squirrel feeder. His own design. His son is a veterinarian and has ordered several of his father's feeders to sell in his clinic."

"I have some news," Kelly piped up. "I got that job I interviewed for a few weeks ago.

"That was the same day your mother was kidnapped wasn't it?" Polly asked.

Kelly looked up feeling everyone's eyes on her. Her mom and dad agreed they weren't going to talk about the WITSEC program unless someone asked specifically about it. Because it had been eleven years, they were remaining in Daytona Beach and Harri and Vicky were keeping the Brookfield name. An article in the local newspaper stated that Harrison Brookfield was going to testify against a man being extradited to California, so the quilters were aware he was testifying about something but they were unaware of the full story.

"Yes, but the interview was before she went missing," Kelly said, snipping a length of pale pink thread to stitch around the petunias in front of her. "I thought for sure I'd blown the interview."

"Why ever did you think that, clever girl like you?" Susan asked.

"I didn't know it at the time, but when I was waiting for the lady, she saw me texting on my cell, and, to my horror, she had checked me out on FaceBook and commented how active I was. Not good."

"But you said you got the job. Your words," Mildred said. "Got the job."

"When she called me last week with the job offer, she told me she was impressed when she happened to see me helping an elderly man in a wheelchair."

"Good for you," Polly said. "Kelly, where's your phone?"

"Oh, it's in my purse. I set it to vibrate if I have a call or a text message. I don't use it very much anymore unless I want to, like if mom calls. Texting maybe once or twice a day. I don't miss it—big waste of time if you don't watch out."

There was a lull in the conversation as each quilter continued to sew—lost in thought.

Mildred looked up at Polly. "What happened to that awful gardener of yours ... Billy?"

"I'm not sure," Polly replied. "When he missed a few days I called him. His phone had been disconnected."

Kelly kept her head down. She knew the connection between Billy and the man who her dad was testifying against for murdering his partner.

"He was arrested, rather his helper was arrested." The quilters looked up at Susan. "I guess I might as well tell you. It's been an awful month. I wish I'd never ... never glanced at one of those dating sites. That day when Polly talked about looking for an escort ... and we dared her ... remember?"

Polly and the other two quilters nodded they remembered, all eyes riveted on Susan.

"Well, I thought I'd take a look ... just for fun mind you. One thing led to another and a gentleman, who turned out to be anything but a gentleman, invited me to meet him for coffee ... as a friend."

"Did you?" Mildred asked her eyebrows raised.

"Well, I didn't think there was any harm in a little conversation over coffee. He stood me up."

Polly, thought back to her date with Sam when she spotted Susan sitting alone sipping a cup of coffee. *I wonder if she told her husband Charlie?"*

"Not only did he stand me up, he robbed me while I was out of the house waiting for him at the coffee shop."

"No!" Polly exclaimed.

"Sounds like he set you up," Mildred said holding her needle in the air.

"He set me up all right. It was that young man helping Polly's gardener. He spotted me as a target while he was working right here in your yard, Polly Pringle."

"Susan, that's awful. But he was quite young. Why did you—"

"Young! He used another man's picture, a very good-looking older man."

"I told you meeting online was dangerous. Didn't I, Polly?" Mildred said with a smug look on her face.

"Well, yes, but you dared me along with Susan. Of course, you also said to prepare myself. We went to that self-defense class together. That class certainly came in handy, I must say."

"We're separated," Susan whispered.

"Oh, Susan, I'm so sorry," Kelly said.

"Thank you, dear. I'm going to divorce him—renew my real estate license."

The other three quilters gasped.

"Polly," Sam called from the kitchen. "Can you come here a minute. I'm not sure where you want this feeder."

"Sam, come meet my quilting friends," Polly called back, thankful for his diversion. Best to save the subject of Susan's travails for the next quilting session.

Sam, a smile on his face, ambled into the dining room and Polly introduced everyone. Sam nodded politely to each in turn.

"That's a really cool feeder, Sam," Kelly said. "Did you paint that little squirrel?"

"Carved and painted, young lady."

"Excuse me, girls," Polly said. "I'll be right back."

Polly and Sam walked out to the backyard leaving Mildred and Kelly grinning from ear to ear at the couple as they chatted about the best location for the feeder. Susan just sat and stared.

"What a nice man," Mildred said. "Polly lucked out. I guess online dating can work, if you're careful," Mildred said looking at Susan. "But, I'm sorry to hear about your problems, Susan."

"She told me it took a few dates before she met Sam. Looks like it was worth trying," Kelly said, taking a stitch with a new color— sunny yellow.

Epilogue

—

Eight Months Later

WAVES GENTLY LAPPED THE white sandy beach bordered by stately palm trees. The temperature was a delightful ninety-two degrees. The bungalow, tucked behind the palms and facing the bay, was cozy yet airy. A fan rotated lazily overhead. Everything was perfect.

Outside, down by the water, Victoria and Kelly, holding each other's hand, laid on their beach towels soaking up the tranquil scene, finally escaping the flurry of depositions. Harri's attorney requested Victoria, and at times Kelly, to be present when Harri was deposed regarding the circumstances surrounding the murder of his business partner and his eyewitness account. Various defense attorneys for Buddy Brown, otherwise referred to as Pit Bull, also requested Victoria's presence at Bull's Grand Jury appearance.

Then the Marshal Service got in the act, along with the California State prosecutors, their staffs, and attorneys. Mr. and Mrs. Brookfield signed the documents releasing them from the Witness Protection Program. The whole process took months and many round trips between Daytona Beach and San Francisco. But with Harri's eyewitness account, along with the set of prints picked up eleven years ago at the crime scene matching Bull's, the case finally went to the jury. Bud Brown, aka Pit Bull, was convicted of murder and was now on death row in San Quentin State Prison.

"Mom?" Kelly squeezed her mother's hand. "Are you asleep?" she whispered.

"No, sweetie. Just resting."

"Do I have time to go to the pool?" Kelly asked.

"You run along. Do you have your cell with you?"

Sitting up on her towel Kelly smiled. "Did you ever think there would be a time you'd ask me that question?"

Shielding her eyes from the sun, Victoria laughed twisting her head to see her daughter. "No, I never did."

"It's in my room. I'll get it. Call me."

"I will."

Kelly ran up to the bungalow and a few minutes later, heading to the pool, waved to her mom.

Victoria stood up, brushed the sand from her legs, and gazed around taking in the beauty of the island. Picking up her towel she strolled up to the bungalow. Before stepping inside she turned and once again admired the white sand and the deep-blue water beyond. Smiling she entered the small house, dropped the towel in the hamper and picked up her filmy white caftan letting it slide over her bronzed body and white bathing suit. Smoothing her black hair, she stepped closer to the front window. Watching. Waiting.

———

THERE HE WAS, LOOKING up at the bungalow, looking at her framed in the window. His foot slipped a little in the sand as his pace quickened. Then running. He caught her in his arms, holding her close.

"Victoria, my beautiful, sweet Victoria. Never again will I let you go."

He kissed her softly, pulled back to look into her eyes, caressing her silky hair. "I love you. I love you with all my heart."

"And my heart is yours, Richard. These last few months … I feared they would never end."

"You're here now, in my arms … I—"

He lifted her chin, kissed her eager lips. He again looked into her warm violet eyes, kissed each cheek, then grasped her hands.

"Is Kelly here?"

"Yes. She's over at the pool."

"Can we walk on the beach a little?" he asked raising her hand to his lips. "I have so much to tell you, but I want to be here when Kelly comes back. I know she and I talked briefly on the phone, but I want her to know I can't wait to meet her."

Pulling him along on the sand, Victoria asked, "What did you find out about the property?"

"First, how long will Kelly be here? I have something I want to run by her."

"Three days."

"How does she feel about us?"

"She's good," Victoria said smiling up at him. "You have to remember she's lived through upheaval before—living a normal life as a five-year-old one minute and uprooted across the country to the opposite coast the next."

"It must have been overwhelming for such a little girl and her mother."

"Harri seemed to pick right up where he left off ... designed a new computer device, started a company, sold it and ended up working as a consultant."

"And that was how he came to have the money he wired to me?" Richard said. "Do you think the police will still come after me for extortion?" he asked.

Victoria laughed. "Pretty clever mister, giving Harri a bogus account number. What if the wire transfer had gone through?"

"No way it could," he said smiling at her.

"No, they won't come after you for possible extortion ... or kidnapping," she said laughing. "That was part of the deal I hammered out with Harri. We dropped the kidnapping charge, and I said Kelly could live with him her last year of school. Of course, the way it's worked out, she's here on spring break and graduates in two months. He wasn't happy, but having Kelly for a little while, telling his colleagues that he had custody, meant everything to him. She'll be with us on some of the holidays and vacation. That probably won't last long once she's in med school."

"Do you think he'll keep his word," Richard asked picking up a seashell, then discarding it.

"I have it in writing. Notarized. Richard, you once said I helped you through those last months in prison when we started corresponding. You did more than help me, my darling. You saved my life."

They stopped walking, waves eddying around their ankles as he drew her into his arms. They didn't speak, just stood holding each other.

They started walking again. "My parents will overlap Kelly's last day here. They had a chance to really get to know each other while we were staying in San Francisco for all the legal meetings. They'll only be here two days."

"So short?"

"They didn't want to intrude—they'll stay longer next time. What's this about Kelly?"

"Montego Bay, here, where we're staying, we only see the guests, other tourists, and the wealthy. But there's another side to the city, and a whole different story—people in shacks, many without running water. There's an orphanage run by a group of nuns. They have a school and welcome all the children who live nearby if their parents will let them. They operate a hospital—all part of the orphanage."

"Can we visit?"

"Yes, but I want to take Kelly with us if she wants to that is. I've been exploring—time hung heavy since the love of my life was occupied elsewhere, and—"

Victoria put her arms around his neck and kissed him, a kiss that turned hot.

"I love you," Richard murmured in her ear.

Her eyes twinkling, she took his hand her toe digging into the sand. "Okay, finish your story about the orphanage."

"You, my love, are a tease. I'll not forget to follow up on that kiss later," he said with a peck on her cheek. Then holding hands they continued walking down the beach.

"The orphanage and the other children who live nearby have very little medical help. A doctor visits once a month."

"That's it?"

"Yep. Anyway, you told me Kelly gets extra credit if she does some community service. I know it's not in the states, but her help would be well documented, and being she wants to enter the medical field, pediatrics, I—"

"You're wonderful. I don't know what she'll say, but it will be interesting to find out. She could stay with us, at least when she's not at the orphanage. Let's head back." Victoria pulled Richard to the water's edge their feet splashing as they walked. "Tell me about the property."

"The building is two stories, pink stucco, in the business district. At first I thought maybe a place on the waterfront, but most of the businesses located there are souvenir shops. So I started looking in the city. It will take some imagination on your part, but I think the site could be a unique spot for a gallery. Tourists flying into Montego Bay, or on a cruise, will spend some time in the city—"

"Have you been painting?" Victoria stopped walking, stood still, holding his hand to her lips as she looked up at him, waiting.

"Yes," he whispered. His voice choked with emotion, "Victoria, maybe you won't like them. Maybe they aren't good enough."

Victoria held his hand to her heart, eyes closed saying a silent prayer of thanks, that he had begun to paint in earnest. She knew he was filled with passion and had the talent to express his passions through his brushes and paints. While waiting between depositions, she had contacted an art dealer in San Francisco. Richard had sent her his sketches of the prisoners, of prison life, so she could feel out the interest of a few dealers. One dealer made an instant offer and wanted to represent Richard when he was ready. He suggested a show at the dealer's gallery featuring Richard as a new talent.

Victoria opened her eyes and looked at the man she wanted to share her life with. Her eyes misted as their plans for the future swam before her—running their gallery in this beautiful Jamaican city on the bay, marketing his paintings to the dealer in San Francisco and hopefully elsewhere, and providing moral support to Kelly through the rigors of med school. But the most important part of her future would be giving her love to this man ... the love of her life ... the Painter.

The End

REVIEW REQUEST

Dear reader, I hope you enjoyed meeting a new friend, Elizabeth Stitchway. If you have the time, it would mean a lot to me if you wrote a review, your honest appraisal. What did you like most? It's super easy. Go to Amazon. Log in. Search: Mary Jane Forbes The Mailbox.

Thank you!

Acknowledgements

Thanks to Joyce Howley and her little dog Regina who prances by my house several times a day. Her big eyes always on alert for squirrels or a feral cat.

A big thanks to Officer David Miller, Port Orange Police Department. His self-defense class for women came in handy in more ways than one. Yes, my rib was bruised but it was well worth it. I encourage every woman to look for a self-defense class in her city.

The book, *WITSEC, Inside the Federal Witness Protection Program*, Pete Earley, and Gerald Shur, 2003, helped me to understand how and why the program started. Case histories were fascinating.

Once again Roger and Pat Grady helped to make sense of the first draft. Thank you.

As ever, thanks to Vera Kuzmyak and Adele Fatigate for their initial feedback.

Thanks to my daughter, Molly, who somehow squeezes a review of my manuscripts into her very busy life. She continues to push me to flesh out the stories.

Social Media. A phenomenon that is fun and useful, but it must be used wisely or it can turn wasteful and even deadly. There's a place for online dating but you have to be smart about it—very smart!

The Painter
The lure of social media—
instant love!

ISBN: 978-0615955452 (sc)
Printed in the United States of America
Todd Book Publications: 7/2011
Second release: 9/2017
Port Orange, Florida

Cover photo: Inga Ivanova
Author photo: Ami Ringeisen
Cover re-design: Mary Jane Forbes 9/2017

Books by Mary Jane Forbes

Bradley Farm Series
Bradley Farm, Sadie, Finn,
Jeli, Marshall, Georgie

The Baker Girl Series
One Summer
Promises

Twists of Fate Series
The Fisherman, a love story
The Witness, living a lie
Twists of Fate

Murder by Design, Series
Murder by Design
Labeled in Seattle
Choices, And the Courage to Risk

Novels
The Mailbox
Black Magic, An Arabian Stallion
The Painter
The Baby Quilt ... a mystery!
The Message...Call Me!
Twister

House of Beads Mystery
Murder in the House of Beads
Intercept
Checkmate
Identity Theft

Short Stories
Once Upon a Christmas Eve, a Romantic Fairy Tale
The Christmas Angel and the Magic Holiday Tree
RJ, The Little Hero

Visit: www.MaryJaneForbes.com

www.ingramcontent.com/pod-product-compliance
Lightning Source LLC
Chambersburg PA
CBHW060809120626
46557CB00001B/139